I0726117

DEATH OF A SORCERER

A LOTUS PALACE MYSTERY

JEANNIE LIN

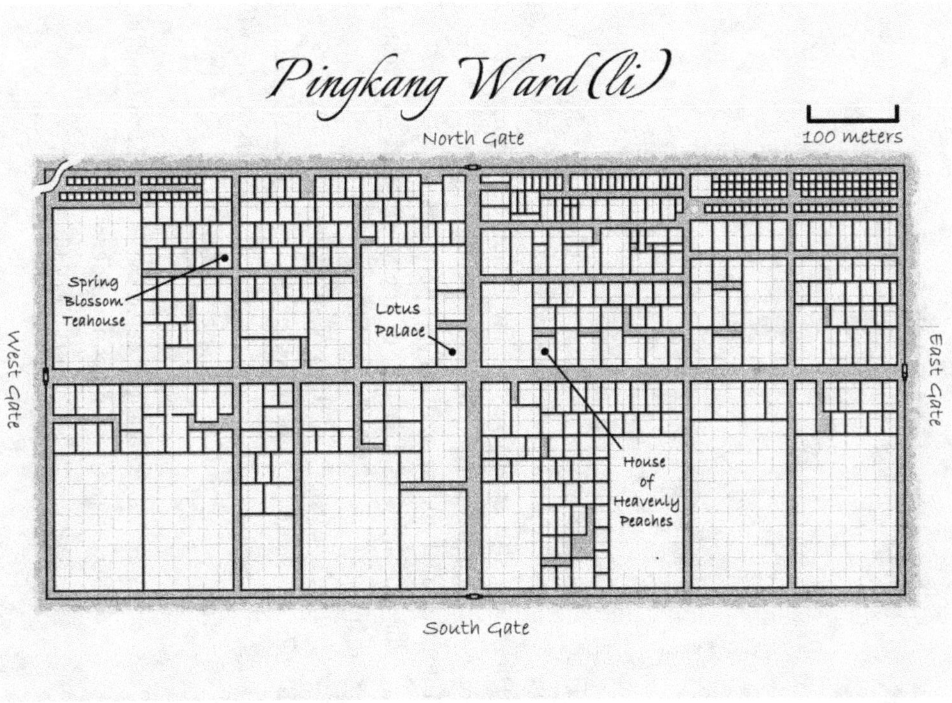
Pingkang Ward (li)
100 meters
North Gate
West Gate
East Gate
South Gate
Spring Blossom Teahouse
Lotus Palace
House of Heavenly Peaches

MAP INFO

The Pingkang ward or Pingkang li is arguably one of the most well-documented sections of the Tang Dynasty capital. There was also extensive documentation on the capital city of Chang'an overall during the Tang era including census information, building permits, and petitions.

The buildings and layout of the ward were re-created using information in this article:

Heng Chye Kiang. (2014). Visualizing Everyday Life in the City: A Categorization System for Residential Wards in Tang Changâan. *Journal of the Society of Architectural Historians, 73*(1), 91-117. doi:10.1525/jsah.2014.73.1.91

This map was designed and created by Jeannie Lin using the Dungeon Scrawl online dungeon builder.

CAST OF CHARACTERS

Note: The family name comes first for characters who have both given and family names listed. I.e. Bai Huang has a given name of Huang and a family name of Bai.

- **Bai Wei-ling** - Known as Wei-wei. The only daughter of the Bai family. Protagonist of *The Liar's Dice* and *The Hidden Moon*.
- **Gao** - A street-smart informer who was appointed constable after saving Li Chen's life. First appeared in *The Lotus Palace*. Protagonist of *The Hidden Moon*.

SECONDARY CHARACTERS

- **Yue-ying** - Former servant in the Lotus Palace pleasure house. Bai Huang's wife and Mingyu's sister. Protagonist of *The Lotus Palace*.
- **Mingyu** - Former courtesan in the Lotus Palace pleasure house. Married to Wu Kaifeng. Yue-ying's older sister. Protagonist of *The Jade Temptress*.
- **Wu Kaifeng** - Former head constable of Chang'an known for his exacting and intimidating demeanor. Mingyu's husband. Protagonist of *The Jade Temptress*.
- **Song Yi** - A courtesan of moderate fame in the pleasure quarter. A member of the House of Heavenly Peaches. She first appears in *The Hidden Moon*. Main protagonist in *Red Blossom in Snow*.
- **Li Chen** - An accomplished scholar and official, he first appears in *The Lotus Palace* as the newly

appointed magistrate and has overseen all of the
investigations in the series. He is also the
protagonist of *Red Blossom in Snow*.

CHAPTER 1

850 A.D. Tang Dynasty China

The thousand-year settlement of Chang'an was a city built upon cities. Temples rested where palaces once stood. One could inhabit the same place where a princess, a villain, a wine merchant had once lived.

Wei-wei had lived most of her life sheltered from the heart of the city. The ward where she lived was occupied by noble families and bureaucrats. Each household was walled away like its own fortress.

The warning Wei-wei's mother had given her when she'd left the family mansion to live in the lower wards of the imperial capital was to be careful.

"There are dangers out in the streets, daughter," Mother had warned.

Wei-wei had been relieved that was all. She'd been afraid Mother was going to provide advice on marriage. Or voice some complaint about her husband, even though Gao stood close enough to overhear. They were at the Bai family mansion, after all. Mother was mistress of the house, free to speak her opinions.

Her mother used few words, so she took care to choose the sharpest ones lest her point be missed. Gao took Mother's disapproving look in stride, bowing solicitously. For someone who had faced the harshness of the street first-hand, her mother's cold glances were mere scratches. Gao also knew, with that uncanny instinct of his, that though his mother-in-law hadn't fully approved of their union, Wei-wei's mother was still—in an odd way—relieved that her wayward daughter was at least finally married.

Wei-wei was happy when she and Gao were finally able to leave the shelter of the family mansion. She had cherished her excursions into the heart of the capital, to the night markets and teahouses. Now she was married, free of the walls that had enclosed her, with the entire imperial city of Chang'an to explore. While Gao patrolled the streets as head constable, she was able to visit the markets, stroll the parks, and go to the temples whenever she pleased.

Wei-wei thought she'd made the transition to lower city life quite well. So when she stepped outside her new home that morning only to have some little scraggly street urchin run by and snatch her purse from her hands, she was in shock.

The skinny thing ran down the lane and disappeared into some nook while Wei-wei stood, flat-footed and staring. There *were* dangers out in the streets. Mother had been right.

A moment later, the boy reappeared to scamper back toward her. He glanced at her, eyes wide, before ducking his head.

"So sorry, Gao Taitai!" he squeaked, not looking at her as he shoved her purse into her hands, then disappeared once more.

After the strange exchange, she raised her parasol to

shield herself from the sun before continuing on her journey. They were in the full of summer and even as early as it was, the day was already warm. She wore the lightest of her robes, adding a pink sash over the layers of pale green silk so as not to attract any wayward spirits.

It was thought that spirits were drawn to single colors, among other things. The superstitions were too many to count, but Wei-wei tried to observe as many of them as she could.

It was the seventh month when the gates of the underworld opened to allow ghosts to wander and visit the living. Today was the middle of the month, the day of the Hungry Ghost Festival, and Wei-wei had made arrangements to go to the temple with Yue-ying, her eldest brother's wife.

Wei-wei waved down a sedan when she reached the end of the lane. Sweat poured down the runner's back as he started toward the Pingkang li, a ward notorious for its courtesan houses. Pingkang was home to the infamous pleasure quarter, where scholars, poets, and bureaucrats came to drink, share stories, and make connections.

Yue-ying's sister Mingyu had once been a celebrated courtesan. She had left that life behind for marriage. Mingyu now ran a teahouse with her husband in the northern part of the ward which was where Wei-wei was headed now.

As the sedan moved through the streets, plumes of smoke rose from several doorsteps. It was customary to put out food to appease any hungry ghosts wandering by and burn ceremonial paper money as an offering.

Wei-wei had put out a bowl of millet with a salted egg on their doorstep that morning. She would wait until sundown to burn joss paper. It was how they had always done it at home. Spirits were supposed to be more active at night.

Now she had her own home where she could carry on the same rituals and traditions her family had observed.

The sedan arrived at the front of the teahouse. Wei-wei paid the runner double his fare to account for the heat and then made her way to the door. Half of the tables inside were full, but there must have been a morning rush of customers as Mingyu sat at a table in the corner, looking exhausted.

Her eyes were closed with her head resting against her hand. Even worn, she looked exquisite. Mingyu's fine-boned beauty was the sort found in paintings. One where every elegant stroke was done with care.

"Elder sister," Wei-wei greeted softly. They were sisters by marriage after all.

Mingyu's eyes fluttered open. "I became so tired all of the sudden," she murmured apologetically.

"Were you up late last night?" Wei-wei asked, seating herself. Now that she lived close by, she made a point to visit the teahouse more often. It had become nearly a second home.

"Not so late. Would you like tea?"

Even as Mingyu offered, she glanced about, looking lost. Wu Kaifeng, Mingyu's tall, dark, and intimidating husband came with the aforementioned tea.

Wu eyed his wife carefully as he set the tray down before them.

"I don't know what this is," Mingyu said, lifting the teapot to pour. "I don't feel sick, but just…out of sorts."

"Could it be some negative influence? Perhaps you've drawn the attention of the s—" It was taboo to speak of spirits or ghosts directly during the month. "Some brothers and sisters," Wei-wei said instead.

There was a superstition that some particularly lustful ghosts might become attracted to the living. Mingyu was so beautiful, even ghosts might want to follow her around.

"You could be with child," Kaifeng said bluntly, never

mind that the strangers sitting at the nearby tables could hear them.

Mingyu's eyes widened as she looked up at him. Wu Kaifeng's expression didn't soften. He had the sort of hard jaw and prominent brow that gave him a permanent scowl, but when Mingyu reached out to touch his hand, their fingers intertwined briefly. An unreadable look passed between them before Kaifeng moved away to tend to their business.

Mingyu still looked tired, but her eyes were bright. "Funny he would be the one to know, while we women were unaware."

"Here I was blaming lustful spirits," Wei-wei said sheepishly, her face burning.

Mingyu laughed.

Yue-ying arrived shortly after. Mingyu's younger sister resembled her in the shape of her face and eyes, though the features were softer on Yue-ying. She might have been overlooked next to her elegant and beautiful older sister, save for one striking characteristic. A deep red birthmark curved along the left side of Yue-ying's face.

Mingyu rose and ushered Yue-ying back into the kitchen where they could speak privately, apparently more discrete than her husband when discussing personal matters. Wei-wei thought to go with them but was caught in-between, uncertain if she was welcome. Though she'd become close to the two of them in the last two years, Mingyu and Yue-ying were sisters by blood. In contrast, Wei-wei had grown up with two brothers and had few friendships outside of her household.

On top of that, the business of children always made her uneasy. She knew so little about it. Pregnancy, birthing them, raising them.

Wu Kaifeng intercepted her partway to the kitchen, engulfing her in his shadow.

"When you go to the market, get this from the herbal shop," he said, holding a paper out to her.

Wei-wei took it reluctantly, taken back by his brusque manner.

"If you could," he added as an afterthought, by way of politeness.

"Of course, Brother Wu."

It never felt appropriate to address him so familiarly. Wei-wei was still inclined to call him 'Constable Wu' as that was how she'd first known him. Wu Kaifeng had held the head constable position before Gao.

She looked over the list of herbal remedies, most of which she was unfamiliar with. Finally, Yue-ying came out of the kitchen.

"It will be just the two of us," she reported. "Mingyu is going to stay and rest."

As they headed out, Yue-ying murmured, "Such happy news."

"Are you certain she's with child?" Wei-wei asked curiously. How could they be certain? Mingyu looked the same to her as she had two weeks ago.

"I felt the same when I was with child," Yue-ying said, taking her arm in a conspiratorial way. "And soon it will be you as well."

The thought seemed to make Yue-ying even happier. The three of them all married and starting families. What greater bond could there be?

Wei-wei wasn't so sure. Not that she wasn't happy for Mingyu. Or for Yue-ying and her daughter, who was a year old now. She just hadn't thought so far. She and Gao were still newly married and he'd never spoken of family. She hadn't either.

Maybe she deliberately tried not to think of such things.

Yue-ying was smiling as they boarded the family carriage. The driver, Zhou Dan gave Wei-wei a nod. She'd known him since childhood. He was a year younger than her and had grown up in their household.

"Lady Bai," he greeted.

"Are you well?" she asked him.

The young manservant gave her a toothy grin. "Getting into less trouble now that you've moved away."

THE EAST MARKET was always an adventure. They entered through the main gate at a crawl surrounded by people and carts on both sides. The lanes inside were arranged in a grid of nine squares, but that was where all orderliness vanished.

The carriage rolled through a wide avenue lined with shops on either end as well as a secondary line of stalls and squatters. On festival days, the market drew in inhabitants from all the surrounding wards, rich and poor.

They stepped off the carriage at a public square and made arrangements to reunite with Zhou Dan after a few hours. Then it was off to their planned destinations.

As expected, the local Buddhist monastery was crowded that day as people stopped by to say a prayer and light incense.

It wasn't that ghost month was a time of fearfulness. It was a time of memorials and awareness of what it meant to live and die. A time to remember those who had come before whose spirits who had no family to support them. The Hungry Ghost Festival finally honored the lost and abandoned.

The main hall of the monastery was clogged with incense

smoke. The cloying scent of sandalwood and camphor surrounded them as they stepped inside.

As Wei-wei stood before the altar, she thought of Gao. Her husband carried his family only in distant memories. His father had died when he was young, and then his mother had been forced to abandon him as well.

On his own from a young age, Gao had done things to survive, he'd told her. She had been afraid to know any more than that. He'd earned a dangerous reputation on the streets by the time she'd met him.

Wei-wei didn't blame Gao. She knew nothing of the hardships of common life growing up within the shelter of her family, surrounded by books. At Gao's core, he was fiercely loyal and protective. He'd opened the world for her and he wanted to do better.

Still, the past could not be ignored. Every action was a seed planted. The ghosts of those Gao had harmed might seek retribution.

That was the heart of the Hungry Ghost Festival. Some souls had been abandoned by the world. Their names were forgotten and they were left hungry without loved ones to tend to them. For one month, when all ghosts roamed free to visit the living, they too needed to be fed.

Beside her, Yue-ying remained silent with her head bowed in prayer. Wei-wei planted her joss sticks into a great brass urn before the altar. Smoke rose from the incense in a great cloud and the scent of it suddenly felt suffocating. Wei-wei escaped from the hall to seek less oppressive surroundings.

Once outside in the courtyard, she breathed in the warm summer air. The faint scent of incense still hovered over her, even outside. There wasn't any place in the city free of smoke that day.

"Wei-wei." Her sister-in-law came up beside her as Wei-

wei stood staring at an arrangement of smooth stones. "Is there something wrong?"

Yue-ying was always observant. She could sense a person's mood without them saying a word.

"Let's go to the market," Wei-wei suggested with forced brightness.

It was a festival day. Why waste it with gloominess?

Outside of the monastery, there was a stall selling amulets carved from peachwood. Wei-wei reached for a small tablet showing an imposing figure with a thick beard and bulging eyes.

"Zhong Kui," the man in the stall explained. He wore gray and his hair was shorn like a monk. "The keeper of ghosts."

Wei-wei ran her thumb over the raised carving. Legend had it that Zhong Kui had passed the imperial examinations in the top position, but was denied the honors due to his ugly appearance. In a rage, he'd thrown his head against the palace gates until he collapsed, dead. In the afterlife, the ruler of the underworld saw Zhong Kui's potential and made him King of Ghosts tasked with hunting down misbehaving spirits and keeping order between the underworld and the land of the living.

The story resonated with her. Zhong Kui had been dealt an injustice in his life. His path was not without error. He'd fallen to rage and despair but had found redemption. If anyone were to understand Gao's path from criminal to head constable, it would be Zhong Kui, the King of Ghosts.

"How much for this?" she asked the vendor.

"Three coppers, good lady," the man replied. He might be dressed as a monk, but he was certainly not one.

Wei-wei started to reach for her purse when Yue-ying made a small noise in her throat.

"Two coppers," Wei-wei countered quickly.

The man cast a sideways glance at Yue-ying before

bowing in acceptance. Wei-wei paid for the amulet and then tucked the wooden carving safely into the pocket of her sleeve.

They went next to the apothecary section and went from shop to shop, gathering the herbs that Wu Kaifeng had listed.

"Ginger is good for nausea. The others are good for bolstering energy," Yue-ying explained.

There was a time when Wei-wei had felt worldly and sophisticated next to her sister-in-law, but that understanding had changed profoundly the more she learned about life outside the mansion, not to mention about family life. Yue-ying had been married for over a year now and was a mother.

They went to purchase joss paper which served as money for the spirits and then went to seek out a few luxuries. Candied lotus seeds and pine nuts. Yue-ying wanted to seek out sugared yam for her daughter and sesame candy for Huang, her husband, and Wei-wei's older brother.

"I'd forgotten my brother liked those," Wei-wei remarked.

Wei-wei was responsible for seeing to her household as well, though it was just her and Gao. His tastes were simple. Sugar was an extravagance he wasn't accustomed to.

The hum and bustle of the festival started to lift her spirits. Wei-wei had always loved festival days. Those were the few occasions when she'd been allowed to go to the marketplaces and parks of the capital, usually under the careful eye of her amah, when she was younger. She and her brother had explored the city, marveling in its many delights.

When they'd gotten older, Huang had been allowed his freedom, while her wings had been suddenly clipped. She was to become a proper girl who would become a proper wife who would become a proper mother.

Wei-wei had a sense that she was far from a proper wife. Apparently, she was a rather scandalous figure in some circles with an even more scandalous husband. Huang had spent his wild student days gambling, drinking, and carousing with courtesans, yet it was she, Bai Wei-ling, the studious middle daughter, who was now considered scandalous?

She'd complained about the injustice of it all to Gao who had laughed. And then he'd kissed her.

"What they say is that you fear nothing," he said, his voice low as he stroked his fingers along her spine. "And that alone in a woman, is scandalous."

It wasn't that she was fearless.

She looked ahead to the public square where a crowd was gathering. Cymbals and drums played, drawing attention to a figure at the center. A sense of anticipation rose from the crowd.

"Precious guests, gather around," a crier hawked. "But not for the faint of heart. What we will show is only for those strong in spirit."

There was a collective gasp from the crowd. What had happened? Wei-wei's feet propelled her forward.

She was afraid of a lot of things. She had just learned to move forward despite the fear.

CHAPTER 2

The center of the attraction was a man with a dark beard dressed in gray robes with a ceremonial headdress. He called himself Daoshi Yu. He was a Daoist master from the foothills of Wudang Mountain.

He had meditated for many years. Communed with the wind and rivers. Communed with the spirits. Fought with the forces of light and dark within his own soul.

As the spectacular introduction continued, a dark and utterly familiar figure patrolled the edge of the crowd. Gao had left that morning to begin his rounds through the East Market. Her husband was easy to find. Gao was loose-limbed, moving quickly and quietly through the crowd. The angles of his face were striking in their sharpness.

Gao wouldn't be considered handsome by most. But he did have a face that made one pause. At first glance, people weren't sure if they found his stark looks compelling or frightening. Most settled on frightening.

A burst of flame billowed from the middle of the crowd.

Wei-wei craned her neck to peer over the heads. What had happened?

The daoshi stood still before them, eyes closed, head bowed.

He was younger than she'd expected. He looked to be thirty years old, the same as her older brother. His hair was coal black and wrapped into a tight coil on his head that was fixed with a wooden hairpin.

The crier boasted that Daoshi Yu had spent years meditating and cultivating his inner qi. The fire had drawn the spirits in the area close and now he was communing with them, paying his respects. The crowd hushed.

"Be careful of pickpockets."

She jumped when Gao spoke in her ear. He had suddenly appeared right beside her.

"Shh!" she hushed. "Be respectful."

He was standing close enough to touch his hand to the small of her back. "Festival days are a favorite time for thieves," he remarked, unrepentant.

Her blood warmed at the daring gesture. Even if they were married. Even if no one could see the touch, such a public display of affection was scandalous.

"But I have nothing to worry about," she teased. "Thieves wouldn't dare touch the constable's wife."

He gave her a questioning look before breaking out in a grin.

Though Gao would never admit such a thing, she knew he had something to do with what had happened that morning. The scraggly urchin must have received some warning to make him return her purse. And with an apology no less.

Gao's dangerous reputation gave her some protection in these streets. But he had earned it at a price.

"I have something for you," she whispered.

"Oh?" His eyebrows raised as she retrieved the amulet of Zhong Kui from her pocket.

"For protection," she explained.

Silently, Gao ran his thumb over the carving. "Against ghosts?" he asked lightly, dark eyes fixing on her.

Her face heated. Did he find her silly for worrying about such things? She herself had nothing to fear from ghosts this month or any month. The spirits who surrounded her were those of her ancestors who were benevolent and well-tended. In life and in the afterlife.

But the spirits that must be following Gao. She and Gao rarely spoke of his past, but she knew he'd fought to survive in the streets for years. He carried a knife. The ghosts that would seek him weren't those of his family. His family was gone.

The spirits of those he'd wronged might want to seek vengeance. The amulet of the King of Ghosts would at least remind them that they were no longer living. They needed to move beyond the suffering of their past lives.

If they couldn't forgive Gao, they could at least move on peacefully. They should spend Ghost Month seeking warmth and consuming food rather than looking for retribution.

"It's just…a good luck charm," she insisted.

With his eyes still on her, he slipped the amulet into his belt. "For good luck then," he said gamely.

Murmurs rose from the crowd. The daoshi had picked up a sword carved out of peachwood from his makeshift altar. He raised it slowly, his lips moving as he chanted in words she couldn't understand. Suddenly, he started waving and spinning the blade all around him, as if he were fighting off a mob of invisible foes.

"Should any malevolent spirits wander here, they will be unable to enter anyone's body while you are under the protection of Daoshi Yu," the crier proclaimed.

Gao coughed beside her. At least she thought it might be a cough.

"Don't get too distracted, Wei-wei. Keep your wits about

you." His fingers caressed across her back as he stepped away. "I have to get back to work."

Gao spared the performance one final look. "At least the ghosts will get to enjoy a good show," he said, before disappearing back through the crowd.

"Your husband is very protective." Yue-ying had returned to her side. "A year ago, I would have never imagined it. Gao, a constable."

A year ago, Wei-wei would have never imagined herself married. Least of all to someone like Gao. She'd been afraid of being married and relinquishing what little freedom she had. She had always dreaded being sent off to a new family and confined to the women's quarters. Newlywed brides were just above servants in a household.

Wei-wei had developed a habit of sneaking out to explore the city. She was certain no noble family would tolerate such behavior. She'd only managed to do so in her family because she'd known how to bend the rules.

But now there were no more rules. Or rather, there existed a whole new set of rules she hadn't yet mastered. The entire city was open to her.

Wei-wei had asked Gao if there were places she should stay away from, to which he'd replied that every place had its own dangers.

"Don't assume anywhere is completely safe," he'd warned her. "But don't show any fear when you're walking through the city. Thieves can sense fear."

Today they were out in broad daylight and surrounded by crowds. County constables were patrolling. As to the ghosts that were said to wander during the seventh month, Daoshi Yu was promising that if they were pure in spirit, there was nothing to fear.

The crier, who was quite impressive in how his voice carried through the market square, was telling them now to be still to not break the master's focus. The daoshi stood tall and straight with his eyes closed. He raised his hands, palms out to the crowd, then turned them downwards to plunge them into the fire.

There was a gasp from the crowd. The man's eyes remained closed, his expression focused. Wei-wei held her breath waiting for him to remove his hands from the brazier. But he held them deep in the flames for what must have been ten counts. Her heart was pounding fearfully by the time he finally pulled his hands free.

The daoshi lifted his hands once more to show the back of his hands and the palms. Unharmed. It seemed the entire crowd let out a sigh of relief.

"Sorcery," murmured a man next to them.

The daoshi's eyes were open now. His onyx pupils glittered as he scoured the crowd. For a moment, they seemed to fix onto her, flashing red before sinking back to black. A trick of the firelight, Wei-wei insisted to herself.

"Is there someone with a knife?" he asked.

It was the first time the daoshi had spoken himself. His voice sounded strangely distant and echoed through the market square. She had no explanation for that. Unlike the crier, he spoke quietly, yet all could hear him.

"I have one," someone replied at the front.

Daoshi Yu lifted a rope from the altar and beckoned the person forward. "Cut through this rope."

The onlooker appeared to be a laborer. He pulled a knife from his belt as he stepped up. The appearance of the naked blade increased the sense of danger. Taking hold of the rope, the spectator cut through it in two quick swipes.

"It's sharp," Yue-ying murmured, unable to take her eyes off the spectacle that was unfolding before them.

"Now, wield it here." The daoshi once again lifted his hands, palms facing out.

The crowd murmured. The man with the knife looked around hesitantly. Daoshi Yi merely nodded.

Wei-wei dug her teeth into her lower lip as the knife flashed forward, slicing across the daoshi's hand. There was no blood, no cry of pain. In disbelief, the man stared at his knife and then did it again, seemingly harder this time. Nothing.

The crowd let out a sound of surprise. There was scattered applause that spread among the spectators. Some laughed in relief.

With his qi in perfect balance, the daoshi claimed he could communicate with the spirits around them. The spirits provided strength and made him impervious to pain or injury.

There were other mystical feats. Daoshi Yu could project his spirit outside of his body which he demonstrated by correctly telling how many coins had been placed inside a closed box when he wasn't looking. When a merchant in the crowd expressed doubt, the daoshi reported the contents inside his bag to his surprise.

It was awe-inspiring. Wei-wei couldn't wait to see what he would show next.

As the daoshi centered his thoughts to focus on the next feat, Wei-wei swore she saw an identical figure, dressed in the same gray robes, walking across the street at the far end of the square. The fire and smoke from the daoshi's brazier stung her eyes. She blinked to clear her vision and when she looked again, there was no one there.

When she looked back at the daoshi, he appeared drained.

"Channeling the spirits has taken all of the daoshi's strength. It is dangerous for him to continue," the crier reported.

Daoshi Yu bowed his head and became still once more.

He was beseeching the spirits to leave him to allow him to regain his strength.

When he opened his eyes again, Yu appeared in a daze. He stumbled as he attempted to take a step.

The crier, apparently a disciple, moved through the crowd to collect coins on behalf of his master. In return, the spectators received stacks of joss paper to burn before their doors to appease the spirits.

"Did you see?" An old woman asked, coming up to Yue-ying. "My son was here watching."

"I didn't see anyone, Auntie," Yue-ying said politely.

"He was right across the street. Walking beside the daoshi." The woman pointed to exactly the spot where Wei-wei had seen the strange, robed figure. "He died a few months ago when his oxcart overturned. But his wounds were gone just now. He looked like my son once more."

Wei-wei's chest hitched. The woman faced the daoshi's altar and bowed before shuffling off, overcome.

"People can see ghosts everywhere when they want to," Yue-ying said when Wei-wei came to her.

But her friend appeared shaken. It was uncommon to speak of such a personal thing as death so openly, but during the Hungry Ghost Festival, it wasn't as taboo.

Wei-wei didn't mention her vision. She had been so shocked by the sight of the daoshi being in two places, both in front of her and down the street at the same time, that she hadn't noticed if there was another figure beside him. It hadn't seemed like anyone on the other side of the street even noticed the figure, now that she thought of it. Her blood ran cold.

The crowd had scattered to move on to other festival offerings, but a few onlookers remained. Daoshi Yu stood now at his altar with a large inkbrush in hand as he scribbled something onto a large yellow strip of paper. A talisman.

Wei-wei had studied some Daoist teachings. At one point, she'd even thought she'd enter a temple instead of getting married. She'd be allowed to surround herself with books and continue her studies. A temple was a perfectly acceptable place for unmarried noblewomen. There were several prominent abbesses in the monasteries of the capital.

She'd spent a few months at a Daoist convent not too long ago. Convents were good places to rest and meditate and wait for gossip to die down after a failed betrothal.

There was nothing about talismans or channeling spirits in any of the scriptures she'd read. There were other stories, though. Fanciful ones written by scholars and exchanged over wine. There were legends filled with sorcery. Stories of immortals and enchanted swords and demons.

"I want to get a talisman for my sister," Yue-ying said, pulling Wei-wei forward with her as if for reinforcement.

"Let's not bother him," Wei-wei said, hesitating.

Something about the man unnerved her. It was the strange vision as well as the way his eyes had seemed to search her out from the crowd.

"Come on," Yue-ying insisted. "We need to keep misfortune away, this month of all months."

CHAPTER 3

Wei-wei stood back as Yue-ying went to the makeshift altar. Daoshi bowed courteously at her approach. His eyes flicked to the red mark on her cheek before returning his full attention to her.

"What are you seeking, Madam?"

"Protection, Master." Yue-ying lowered her voice. "For my sister. She's newly with child."

The daoshi looked to Wei-wei. "She is your sister?"

"No—not her."

"But she *is* your sister," he said evenly.

Yue-ying frowned, then her eyes lit up. "Daoshi Yu is correct. She's my husband's sister."

"But not the one who requires protection," he said with a knowing look.

He dipped his large brush into a bowl of red ink before setting it on the paper. His arm moved in a sweeping pattern, tracing out a snakelike design. Curious, Wei-wei stepped closer.

The writing was unintelligible, though it looked like there

were characters embedded within the scrawl. The daoshi wrote in one continuous motion without lifting the brush.

"These are not hanzi characters, Honorable Lady."

Wei-wei looked up abruptly to see the man's eyes fixed on to hers. His brows were thick, meeting close over the bridge of his nose. The eyes themselves were also distinctive. She was close enough to see that his pupils looked particularly large.

Wei-wei hadn't realized she had leaned in so close and abruptly took a step back.

"The lady sees things that others do not see," he declared, his gaze remaining on her.

Wei-wei didn't know how to respond. His directness was unsettling when combined with the strange vision she'd just witnessed. She was filled with a mixture of fearful curiosity.

"The symbols go beyond the words of mankind," he went on. "To speak to the forces of heaven and earth, body and spirit."

He set his brush down. With careful hands, he lifted the talisman and presented it to Yue-ying with instructions to post the inscription above Mingyu's door to protect those within.

"And for you, Honorable Lady?" he asked after Yue-ying thanked him.

Wei-wei shook her head and tried to politely take her leave.

"I see a child. A son," he interrupted.

She was taken aback. "I don't have a son."

"This child is not yet of this earth. I see him only in shadow."

A shudder went down her spine. Vaguely, she sensed Yue-ying moving closer.

"There are forces keeping him from coming to you," the

daoshi continued, relentless. "A great imbalance that must be righted."

"Wei-wei," Yue-ying murmured in warning, tugging at her arm.

She should have walked away. This man was a stranger and speaking of inappropriate things. But lurid curiosity had its fingers wound around her, holding her in place.

Daoshi droned on, as if in a trance. "Debts. Soul-debt, that must be paid—"

"I have no debts," she blurted out, heart racing. She'd never wronged anyone.

"Not yours."

The daoshi's black gaze fixed on her. She had the sense that he wasn't so much looking at her, but looking into her with his eyes piercing through her skin like sharp needles.

Then, all of the sudden, the fervor that had gripped the master faded. He blinked a few times, as if coming out into the sun from a dark room. Calmly, he picked up his brush and drew out a cryptic and looping symbol in red ink on a strip of yellow paper. The last part of the symbol stabbed suddenly downward, ending like the point of a knife.

"Lady," he said courteously as he held out the paper to her. "For you. And for those close to you."

Gao. She thought of her husband who walked through dark shadows and corners, unafraid. She knew he'd seen death. He had touched it. If there was such a thing as soul-debt, Gao would be the one to owe.

Wei-wei stared at the yellow paper uncertainly. A breeze coursed through the square and the banner rippled like a snake in the daoshi's hands.

Finally, she reached for it. He was a daoshi, one who had studied the way, and likely more knowledgeable about such mysteries than she. That must explain why he was so bold and so strange.

It would have been rude to just walk away, but there was more than politeness holding her there. Wei-wei hated to admit it, but part of her was afraid to dismiss him. Wei-wei looked to the spot across the square where she'd seen *something* during the daoshi's performance. She'd felt something as well and seen a strange gleam in the man's eyes that she couldn't explain.

As she reached out to take the talisman from the daoshi, a dire feeling crawled over her. A warning whisper sounded in her ear.

This was the month of ghosts and the month of signs. And bad things happened to people who ignored signs.

Wei-wei looked up from her book at the sound of footsteps at the door. The sky through the window had gone dark and there was an impatient hissing and bubbling from the pot on the stove which reminded her that it had been a while—how long had it been since she had left the rice cooking?

She rushed to her feet and lifted the lid just as Gao came through the door.

"Smells good," he remarked as she stabbed a wooden spoon into the rice, holding her breath as she stirred toward the bottom.

Not burnt.

She exhaled with relief. "It's late," she said turning around.

Gao shrugged. "Not so late."

She had expected Gao would be required to patrol the streets a little later into the evening on festival days, but ghosts were said to be more active at night. Especially when the moon was full as it was tonight. Mother had always made a point to usher Wei-wei and her brother inside by sundown during the seventh month. Of course, they had been children then and it was more of a family tradition than a true cautionary measure.

She didn't want Gao to think of her rituals as childish. He'd raised his eyebrows but said nothing when she'd set out dishes on their doorstep to provide food and drink for wandering ghosts at the start of the month.

It was a luxury to have extra food to offer in such a manner and Gao had known what it was to go hungry, while her family never thought twice about putting out food that would never be eaten.

She readied the dinner table while Gao unfastened his headdress and removed his belt. The first time she'd seen him in the constable's uniform, she had thought he must have stolen it. Even now, after more than a year in the position, the rigid lines of the uniform still didn't quite suit Gao.

A constable was meant to be a figure of authority. Constables enforced the rules and reminded others to stay in line. Gao was nothing so rigid and structured. Her father had once been stationed to the north. She'd seen a wolf once roaming in the highlands as the day faded into dusk. Rangy, and dark-furred, with a dangerous and sleek sort of beauty. That was what Gao was like. He was a lone force in the city.

"What's this?" he asked mildly as she scooped rice into two ceramic bowls.

He held up the yellow paper marked vividly with red ink.

"It's a talisman from that Daoist master from the market."

That raised eyebrow again. "How much did he charge for it?"

Heat rushed up the back of her neck. "Nothing. He didn't want any money."

Something about Gao's skeptical tone made her bristle. Wei-wei set the bowls down on the table and added a dish of stewed greens and pickled vegetables.

"What is it supposed to do?" Gao asked mildly as they sat.

"I don't know. For protection or something like that."

"Something like that," he echoed vaguely.

She set down her bowl a bit too forcefully. "I didn't ask for a talisman. The daoshi just handed it to me."

Gao blinked at her, taken aback. She didn't know why she was so upset either. She'd considered burning the paper on the way home. There were plenty of braziers set out to burn paper money for the spirits. But then she wondered if she would be committing some taboo burning a daoshi's talisman. In her world, writing held a certain power, and the strange red character Daoshi Yu had written out seemed to carry some hidden covenant she didn't dare break.

"Let's eat," she urged sullenly, not wanting to be in a mood, but unable to shake it.

Gao, in contrast, seemed particularly agreeable. "It's very good," he said between mouthfuls.

"Yue-ying was here. She cooked everything."

"What did she put in this?"

"Just…salt."

Gao nodded approvingly and continued eating. He was always hungry and not particular about food. He never complained about anything she cooked, even on the days when she lost track of time and burned their dinner.

She glanced over to the talisman abandoned on her writing table before turning her attention back to Gao. They had wed over a year ago and the days had been strange and new and happy. For the first time in her life, she existed outside of the boundary of her family. She had a home of her own without servants to keep things in order.

As for Gao, he'd been alone nearly all of his life. Lucky to sleep beneath a roof, he'd told her once. Her heart broke to think of him like that. Cold. With no one beside him.

The two rooms they lived in now were an unspeakable luxury for him, a fraction of the size of the Bai family mansion for her. Gao had been accountable to no one, she had been surrounded by family and servants all her life.

They had come together under unusual circumstances, questioning nothing. Asking little of one another. They had married without the usual promises. Gao was without family to make arrangements on his behalf. Their lives together were unmapped.

Yet sometimes, because she had a mind full of questions, she wondered. What would their future look like? What did Gao want it to look like?

"Mingyu is with child," she announced tentatively.

Gao paused to nod in acknowledgment. He knew Mingyu and her husband. Wu Kaifeng had been head constable before Gao.

Seeing Gao's bowl was nearly empty, Wei-wei picked up some greens with her chopsticks to give to him. It was a wifely gesture, something she'd seen her mother do for her father when they had the opportunity to share a meal.

"It made me think." Why were there butterflies in her stomach? She swallowed. "Yue-ying has a daughter now and Mingyu is expecting. I wondered if you ever thought —if we…"

For once, Gao seemed uncertain as well. "Are you…?"

"No."

"Oh."

Their simple meal was nearly done. They ate in silence during which Wei-wei focused intently on the bottom of her bowl. She was interrupted by the gentle stroke of Gao's thumb over her knuckles.

She looked up to see him watching her, his expression as soft as she'd ever seen it.

"I'd always thought what would come would come," he said, his voice husky.

She didn't know if Gao was talking about them or life in general.

"What if…what if it's not possible?"

Gao frowned. "Why wouldn't it be possible?"

It was difficult to speak of such things to Gao. These matters were difficult to speak aloud to anyone. He was her husband, but he was a man. And for all her learning, she didn't have the words to explain this. She didn't even know if there was anything worth explaining.

"The daoshi said something. About balance. About things that might prevent a child from coming to us."

Her face flushed as she remembered the dark proclamation. The daoshi had talked about a boy who he insinuated was meant to be her child. Hers and Gao's.

Gao didn't scoff at her. Instead, his look of concern deepened.

How could she explain to him that this was one of her worries? Her mother had such a difficult time conceiving and giving birth. Mother's difficulties had only been hinted at in whispers, but Wei-wei had been keenly aware of it.

Mother had been unable to give Father more sons. As a result, Father had taken a concubine at her mother's behest. Later, he'd come home with a young boy that Wei-wei had only heard about in passing.

The boy was her brother. They shared a father, but not mothers. Though everything had been agreed upon, even orchestrated by her mother, the events had caused a tear in the fabric of their family, one that she wasn't certain had ever been fully mended.

She had never spoken about her fear of the same thing happening to her to anyone. Then to hear such ominous words from this stranger.

"Wei-wei," he began quietly. His fingers curled around hers. "Wei-wei, that man was a charlatan."

"There were things that happened. He was able to do things."

"There are acts like that on every street. Don't spare him another thought."

She shook her head, uncomfortable in her own skin all of the sudden. The daoshi wasn't the point. Whether or not he was genuine wasn't the point, but she didn't know how to explain herself to Gao so he didn't know what the problem truly was. She didn't know either.

"He put his hands into the fire," she tried to explain. She told him about the other feats. How the daoshi had been impervious to pain. How a sharp knife had failed to cut him. And then he'd said something spooky to her about a child whose spirit couldn't come to her. And soul debt.

At the moment, it had all felt starkly true.

"Did you know the man who tried to cut him?" Gao countered. "Was he someone you'd seen in the market before?"

She thought about it. The man who'd come from the crowd was unfamiliar to her, but Chang'an was such a large city.

"Were you approached by someone else?" Gao pressed. "Someone who was convinced by what they'd seen?"

There had been that old woman. The one who said she'd seen a vision of her deceased son.

"It's a common ploy," Gao explained. "They work together, but you wouldn't know it."

Wei-wei thought it over. It made sense the way he explained it, but she had been so certain of what she'd seen.

"The knife was sharp enough to cut through rope."

"It's easy to fool the eye if you're distracted. Here—" Gao spread his hand flat onto the table before her. Suddenly he drew a knife and plunged it directly into the back of his hand.

She shrieked and shot to her feet in horror.

Gao was immediately beside her, wrapping his arms around her as she tried to look at his hand. It was untouched.

"Don't do that!" she snapped.

"I didn't mean to scare you."

She punched him in the shoulder as he gathered her close.

"I'm sorry," he soothed.

Her heart was pounding even as her knees wobbled with relief. She sank her head against his chest. "You're horrible."

"I am."

His heart beat steadily beneath her ear as he held her. He ran a steady hand up and down her spine, drawing the tension from her limbs.

"Horrible," she echoed.

She could barely remember what had started the conversation, but Gao remembered.

"Tricksters like that prey on your fears," he said. "They have ways of searching them out."

Wei-wei closed her eyes. "When I think back on it now, he never said any of the things I thought he'd said."

He'd barely made any sense at all. The daoshi was a showman. He had pounced on her confusion and her mind had made its own meaning.

"Whatever happens will be between you and me and the heavens," Gao said against her hair. "No one else knows anything."

He kissed her then, gently. And then put out the lanterns before taking her to bed.

CHAPTER 4

Gao was not surprised the next morning to hear of the complaints from the marketplace. There was a trickster, a charlatan, a fraud. Someone swindling people out of their money.

"Was he presenting himself as a Daoist sorcerer?" Gao asked the merchants.

Of course, he was.

The complaints ranged from bilking a few taverns out of food and drink to performing exorcisms throughout the city for a fee.

There was nothing to be done for such petty schemes. People had willingly paid the daoshi for his services and it couldn't be proven that the talismans and rituals didn't work. In light of the other rackets being run in Chang'an, these scams were minor.

But this trickster had used his lies on Wei-wei. Gao wanted to tell the man a few things about that.

It was only a matter of hours before Gao located the seedy inn where the sorcerer was said to be lodging. The building had two levels and was buried at the end of a lane just outside the East Market. Shuttered and dark, it was exactly where rats might hide.

Gao had assumed the sorcerer and his cronies would be quick to leave town, having collected a large amount of money, but he was supposedly still in his room.

After one knock and then a louder attempt, the door remained shut. Unmannered as he was, Gao pushed the door open to reveal the sorcerer sitting upright and cross-legged just inside.

The man's eyes were closed and he sat with his spine straight and hands rested palms up over his knees. Gao took a step into the chamber and the man remained in the same meditative pose.

Could Wei-wei have been right? Maybe he was a daoshi, a master after all. Gao had never seen anyone enact such serene stillness.

He quickly realized why.

The sorcerer wasn't meditating. He was dead.

No one would touch the body.

The yamen runners he called to the task shrank away when they saw the strangeness of the death. The innkeeper started burning incense and ran out to seek *another* exorcist to cleanse away the lingering spirit of this sorcerer's sudden death.

Cursed ghost month. It made the task of dealing with the dead even more difficult.

Aside from rampant superstition, there were practical challenges. the body had grown rigid in a seated position. It wouldn't fit through the door.

Gao stationed a constable at the door to stand guard. The corpse wagon to transport the body to the coffin house remained at the far end of the lane, blocking any onlookers from venturing too close. There were a few curious enough to try, despite the threat of hungry, wandering ghosts.

Gao eased himself past a group huddled close together, whispering. The sorcerer had misused dark forces and paid a price. The more respectable portion of the crowd scattered hastily as he passed through. He had to sidestep a bamboo parasol that nearly caught him across the face.

The walk to the Pingkang ward took up half the hour. He made his way to the tea house at the north end and came to a stop.

A bright yellow paper with a red ink symbol had been pasted over the door.

Inside, the proprietor did not look happy to see him. But Wu Kaifeng rarely looked happy. The man was uncommonly tall and his gaze uncommonly sharp.

It had once been said that in the streets, everyone feared Gao and Gao feared Wu Kaifeng. It wasn't entirely untrue. When Wu Kaifeng had been head constable, Gao had the good instinct to stay out of his way.

Now Gao knew him well enough to understand that Wu was willing to provide advice if asked directly. Gao pulled Wu outside before describing the situation.

"Wait a few hours, the limbs will loosen," Wu replied with brutal efficiency.

He hadn't known that. Gao, like most people, stayed far from the dead, but Wu Kaifeng had more experience as a constable and examiner than anyone he knew.

"There wasn't any visible mark on him," Gao went on. "He looked like he was sleeping, but sitting upright."

"Some deaths cannot be explained," Wu said simply.

"The man was too young to just die in his sleep."

Wu didn't blink. "Why would that be?"

Gao paused at that. Wu was right. He was making too

many assumptions. There would be a more thorough examination once the body could be transported to the coffin house.

As he prepared to leave, his eye was once again drawn to the paper above the tea house door.

"That talisman," he began.

Wu glanced up. "Mingyu's sister brought that here. She said that infants in the womb are vulnerable to wandering spirits."

Wu didn't sound particularly worried. For many, the folk rituals around ghost month were just accepted and practiced as a custom.

Gao was reminded of his conversation with Wei-wei. "My wife told me of your news…I should say…congratulations."

The corner of Wu's mouth lifted in an uncharacteristic and measured show of…happiness?

An awkward silence followed. It was easier for men like them to speak about death than the niceties of family life.

Gao left quickly after that to see to the body of the sorcerer.

It was still too rigid to get out of the door, which gave him time to question the innkeeper. When did the daoshi come to the inn? Did he have visitors? What were his comings and goings?

Another room in the inn had been vacated early. The lodger hadn't informed the innkeeper he was leaving, even though the room was paid for through the week. An accomplice? Maybe. Or just one of the thousands of people who went in and out of the East Market and surrounding wards every day.

Gao attempted to find out when the sorcerer had last been seen. A tour of the stalls and drinking houses yielded a set of conflicting stories. Daoshi Yu had performed a ghost clearing ceremony in front of a tavern at sundown. Then he claimed he needed to rest to regain his strength and retired to his rooms. But someone had seen him late that night drinking down the street. Someone else swore they had seen him early that morning, stumbling through the streets before the morning drums.

By the time Gao saw him in his room, it would be several hours later, completely cold.

Gao returned to the rented chamber to find that the constables had failed to inspect and search through the man's belongings.

None of them wanted to be inside the room with the body, so Gao had to see to it himself.

"Sir, are you certain?" one of his men asked nervously as Gao started toward the room.

He stopped. "What's the problem?"

"He moved," the younger constable said, his face pale.

Gao looked back to the sorcerer who was still seated rigidly on a bamboo mat just inside the door. Other than his gray pallor going grayer, he looked the same.

"Wen An saw it too," the constable insisted.

It was a trick of the eye. If you stared at something long enough, it would seem to move. For instance, Gao did, at that moment, think that he saw a twitch beneath the sorcerer's eyelids.

"He's dead," Gao reminded them, agitated.

He stepped into the chamber and refrained from passing his hand beneath the still figure's nose. He had already examined the body the first time. No breath, no pulse. Icy to the touch. Dead.

Gao found a travel pack along with a few rusted coins and a sword carved of peachwood. There was a stack of yellow papers and a dish of red cinnabar to be used for ink.

He stuffed any materials he found back into the bag. He would review the contents once he was outside of the room.

Maybe the presence of the body, sitting so serenely in the middle of everything, was starting to affect him as well.

It was hours before the body could be moved. Gao hired laborers to do the dirty work and was glad to be free once the wagon rolled off.

As the other constables retired for the evening, he overheard them talking about burning incense at a temple to cleanse away any evil spirits that might linger. They had kept apart from Gao since he'd come out of the chamber with the sorcerer's belongings.

Don't worry, he wanted to tell them sarcastically. *I have a ghost-slaying amulet.*

Whether or not one was devout, the month and the festival scraped open hidden fears and old guilt. Had one done enough for their loved ones? For their ancestors? Did one have wrongs weighing on their soul that needed to be made right?

Gao wasn't completely unmoved by such beliefs. He reached into the pocket of his robe to draw out the wooden amulet Wei-wei had given him. Zhong Kui, the King of Ghosts, who looked practically like a demon himself. Gao kept it on him, not because he believed the trinket had any power, but because Wei-wei had given it to him. She was the only person who cared for him. Not just for his safety but for —his soul.

He had no family left. Before Wei-wei came into his life, he hadn't adhered to any rituals showing respect to the ancestors. All of the spirits in his line were left untended. He had nothing but wandering ghosts peering over him, abandoned and hungry.

"A trick knife?" Wei-wei asked.

Gao was going through the satchel he'd taken from the sorcerer's room and describing the items to his wife so she could write them into the report for the magistrate's records. Over the last year, he'd mastered enough characters to plod through rudimentary reports on his own, but this was a more complicated case and Wei-wei was so much faster. The tip of her brush glided over the paper faster than a hummingbird's wings.

"Take a look." He held up the knife so she could see. "The edge is sharp, but the tip collapses."

Wei-wei's eyes narrowed on him in warning, recalling his shocking trick from the night before. He pushed back the point of the blade lightly before handing the fake weapon over to her. She set her writing brush against the holder before taking it.

"I feel so foolish," Wei-wei said, pressing the tip to her palm and watching it disappear. "It was all staged. Like a play."

"And what about this?"

The next item he pulled from the satchel was a dried gourd with a stopper. When he shook it, it sounded as if there were some powder inside.

"*Huo yao*," Wei-wei read from the inscription etched on the outside.

Fire medicine?

"Many Daoists search for an elixir of immortality," Wei-wei surmised. "This might be some alchemical mixture."

"Maybe this is what killed him?" Gao pulled the stopper to sniff at the contents while Wei-wei made a sound of alarm.

"Don't do that," she scolded. "It could be poison."

"It smells like charcoal," he reported with a shrug, putting the stopper back on.

The rest of the contents inside the bag were the ink brush and a bundle of talisman paper, rolled together and tied with string. There was no money other than the three rusted coins he'd found earlier.

Wei-wei resumed her writing, but paused when she reached the end. She frowned, looking troubled.

"Is this upsetting you?" he asked.

Wei-wei didn't like to be sheltered or have details hidden from her. She wanted to hear about his day and the only thing she liked more than asking a question was asking ten questions. But most of his days weren't so gruesome and Wei-wei had just spoken to the deceased the day before.

"I'm just thinking." She twisted the calligraphy brush in a slow circle between her fingers as she read through the report once more. When his wife pondered over something, her eyes took on a faraway expression. She became completely absorbed.

"You said that there were many complaints against the daoshi."

She preferred to refer to the dead man by the more respectable term.

"Yes, throughout the market."

"Complaints about him scrounging drinks and charging people to exorcise every chair and table."

Gao fought a smile as he nodded. He hadn't said it quite so colorfully.

"It just seems a very different approach from what I saw."

"He seemed to be a man of many schemes."

Wei-wei wasn't satisfied. "He wouldn't take payment from me or Yue-ying. He made it seem as if the money didn't matter. He also made it seem…" she paused, thinking. "You said tricksters know how to play on our fears. I think Daoshi Yu also knew how to play on our hopes."

"How do you mean?"

"He recognized that I could read hanzi. He said I could see things that others didn't. It was flattering."

"He was drawing you in," Gao observed, his hands tightening into fists before he reminded himself that the object of his anger was already dead.

"I'm certain we were approached with a purpose, Yue-ying and I. We were led to believe that we had decided to go to the daoshi on our own, but a woman stopped us as the rest of the crowd was breaking away. What she said sparked curiosity and made us linger."

The trickster knew to target women of means. Yue-ying had married into the wealthy Bai family and though Wei-wei was no longer rich, having married the likes of him, she still wore the signs of her upbringing.

Gao had known Wei-wei came from wealth the first time he'd seen her. Even though it had been in the middle of the night and it had been dark. Just the tilt of her head and the tone of her voice told him enough.

"All these illusions. Hidden accomplices. There must be

more to this than petty thievery." Wei-wei concluded. "Daoshi Yu was seeking something more."

Wei-wei was out of place in the city, as much as he was out of place standing beside her. There was an advantage to being out of place. His wife was uncannily perceptive at times. They were ill-matched, yet somehow perfectly suited.

"The only complaints I hear about are from the street," Gao remarked. "Any word of a more elaborate scheme would come to someone with much more authority."

"Li Chen?" Wei-wei suggested.

He nodded. "I'll go to the magistrate."

RICH PEOPLE WERE TOO TRUSTING.

Gao knew this because Wei-wei trusted him. He also knew this because the magistrate trusted him, despite his reputation for being a low-life hustler from the alleyways of Pingkang.

If the sorcerer had cheated anyone wealthy enough to matter, the complaint would have gone to Li Chen.

Li wasn't in the magistrate's compound, which meant he could only be in one other place. Gao traveled once more to Pingkang, arriving just as the evening lanterns were being lit. Paper orbs glowed from the rafters of the illustrious courtesan houses of the quarter.

The pleasure houses looked best at night, when the lanterns cast a warm, inviting light in the parlors and the shadows hid the faded paint and worn edges. Music could be heard just beyond the flutter of the curtains.

Gao had never frequented the courtesan houses. Their talents were meant to attract wealthy and powerful men. For most of his life, he was so poor that he didn't know what a purse was. One required two coins to require something to hold them in.

He wasn't headed to the center of the pleasure quarter this evening. Instead, he made his way to an intersection located off the main thoroughfare. The square was surrounded by several small shops as well as food stands. He passed by the moderately-sized courtesan house. The establishment served as an anchor in the neighborhood, feeding into the surrounding stalls and venues like the tea house that stood on the opposite side of the street.

At the tea house, Gao carved a direct path up the stairs. Seated at a small table set up against the window was Magistrate Li Chen. He'd changed out of his state robes, but he was easily recognizable, nonetheless.

When paintings depicted proper scholar-gentlemen, they looked like Li Chen. The various lords and bosses of the underground betting houses had laughed when they saw Li Chen was the newly appointed magistrate. He was youthful, unassuming, and had come from some quiet, rural jurisdiction.

Then it turned out Li Chen had a habit of employing fearsome lawmen and possessed a methodical, untiring dedication toward the pursuit of justice. He also could not be bribed.

The magistrate was looking out the window as Gao approached and was startled when he turned back to see Gao standing over him.

"Constable…has something happened?"

"It's Chang'an. Something is always happening."

Gao pulled out the stool and seated himself opposite the magistrate, resting his elbows on the table.

Li Chen regarded him with a frown. "It must be important, or you wouldn't have come here."

"There was a body discovered in an inn outside the East Market."

"Yes, I received your preliminary notice. Mysterious circumstances, you said?"

"He was moved to the coffin house late today." Gao slid the report across the table. "He was presenting himself as a daoshi with the purpose of swindling money from others. I wondered if you had heard of any related cases."

Li Chen reached for the report and quickly read through the first pages.

"Daoshi Yu," he read.

"He was performing in the market during the festival. A display of Daoist sorcery apparently with fire and illusions."

"It's not illegal to claim special powers," Li mused. "There are magical elixirs being sold on every lane."

"My wife witnessed the show. She thinks the sorcerer may have had some larger scheme in mind. Perhaps it led to his death."

Li Chen thought for a moment. "There's a money purification scheme that has come up here and there over the past year."

The magistrate described how the scheme involved convincing someone that their money had become tainted with dark energy or possessed by malignant spirits. Usually, it was used to explain a recent bout of misfortune.

"In order to remove the curse, the afflicted person must hand over their money to be cleansed. The swindler typically promises the money will be returned after some ritual is complete."

"Clever in its simplicity," Gao remarked.

"Those who are taken by it are usually too ashamed to lodge a complaint. I can see how, during this month, such schemes might take on a more personal bent, exploiting those who are in mourning or grieving over recent losses. It's unconscionable."

Li's expression hardened in a rare display of anger. A moment later, the anger faded into his usual neutral demeanor. "But we don't know that this daoshi was involved in any such schemes. We must investigate the cause of his death without judgment. The examiner should be able to give us his report tomorrow."

Magistrate Li paused to drink his tea. As he did so, his eyes involuntarily wandered once more out the window. Gao followed the direction of Li Chen's gaze to the courtesan house across the square.

The magistrate quickly turned back to their conversation. "Thank you for bringing this information to me, Constable."

Gao looked Li Chen squarely in the eyes. To Li's credit, he didn't waver.

"How did you know to find me here?" Li asked after a thought.

Gao shrugged. "A lucky guess."

Li Chen said nothing and drank more tea.

Gao had a reputation for being able to get information from people. It really wasn't because everyone feared him, as many assumed. It was just that people weren't particularly good at hiding things. It was as if they wanted someone to know.

A woman's voice floated across the street. Li Chen couldn't resist glancing down to the entrance of the courtesan house. Apparently, the young lady there wasn't the one that he'd come to admire.

Gao couldn't fault Li for his routine of coming to the tea house to pine. Gao himself had started down this business of being constable to impress a woman. Here he was, still at it a year later.

"That's The House of Heavenly Peaches, isn't it?" Gao asked.

"Perhaps it is…I'm not certain."

Li Chen was certain. Gao had seen him there a year ago, calling on one of the courtesans in a private parlor. The man should never attempt to lie. He was awful at it.

"Why do you ask?" Li wondered.

"Just conversation."

Gao had just noticed over the entrance, cast in shadow from the placement of the lanterns, was a yellow paper with red writing.

It wasn't Wei-wei's first time at the House of Heavenly Peaches. Or even her second time, which is how Wei-wei convinced Gao that it would be easy for her to call there that morning.

Having the fearsome head constable striding in to ask questions would set everyone on guard. Wei-wei could speak more freely to the ladies of the house and find out what they knew about Daoshi Yu.

She pulled the bell at the door and waited. And waited.

The street was empty at this early hour and she remembered that the inhabitants of the courtesan house were probably up late entertaining the night before. She should have waited an extra hour or two before bothering them.

She was about to leave when the door creaked open. Wei-wei was delighted to see a familiar face.

"Miss Song Yi," she greeted brightly. "It's been a long time."

The courtesan blinked at her. Song Yi's face was unpainted and she appeared younger than Wei-wei remembered.

Wei-wei had first come to the Heavenly Peaches disguised as her younger brother. She and Song Yi had later met without the disguise and the courtesan had been kind enough not to question her as to why she'd been pretending to be someone she wasn't.

"I thought I would come by as a courtesy…and see how you were doing." She probably should have thought longer on her reasons for calling at a courtesan house.

"Lady Bai," Song Yi replied, drawing out the greeting. "How kind of you."

"I've brought a gift for your house," Wei-wei offered. "Tea. From Yunnan."

A faint, confused smile touched the courtesan's lips. "Do come in," she said, conceding that she had little choice in the matter.

Song Yi managed to carry herself with a stately elegance despite being caught unprepared. She led Wei-wei inside, seating her in the main parlor.

"Auntie, can you bring tea?" Song Yi called out to what seemed like the empty room.

A face with glittering black eyes peered out through a set of curtains. It was the elderly courtesan who, from what Wei-wei recalled, disapproved of everything.

"Old Auntie," Wei-wei greeted cheerfully, remembering how the woman was addressed.

Old Auntie sniffed and cast a dismissive wave her way before disappearing. Wei-wei didn't think there would be any tea coming.

"What brings you here, Lady Bai?" Song Yi smoothed her robe over her knees as she seated herself.

"Oh, just a friendly visit."

It probably wasn't often or ever that ladies came to visit the courtesan house. Wei-wei tried to mimic Song Yi's elegant poise, running her hands over her lap to smooth out her robe. She really wished there was tea.

"I heard you were to be married to the magistrate," Song Yi offered as the pause in the conversation grew overly long.

"No. No, we didn't. We weren't—"

How could anyone have heard that? She and Li Chen had worked hard at not becoming betrothed.

"I thought that maybe that was why you…would come to see me," Song Yi explained. "I assure you, the magistrate isn't here. Li Chen hasn't come by in a long time."

She had completely forgotten. Magistrate Li and the courtesan had been engaged in some sort of thing. He at least had come to visit her several nights in a row.

"I'm not here looking for Magistrate Li," Wei-wei began. She should have just let Gao throw his authority about. "I was just wondering about the talisman. The one over your door. Did you get that from a man calling himself Daoshi Yu?"

Song Yi's eyes widened with alarm. "Lady Bai, he didn't...."

Wei-wei stared at her. "Didn't what?"

"He didn't do anything unspeakable to you, did he?"

Unspeakable. Wei-wei hated that word. That nothing of a word that became the sum of all the worst possibilities. So much worse than just speaking.

"He gave me a talisman," Wei-wei recounted. "And warned me I had soul-debt to atone for."

"Debt." Song Yi's eyes flashed angrily. "That old game. He tried the same thing with Pearl. You weren't seduced by all of his talk of balancing yin and yang, were you?"

"Seduced?"

"We bought the talisman hoping to ward away misfortune and attract prosperity. Things have been difficult here since...." She paused and thought better of what she had meant to say. "After we put that paper up, the daoshi showed up here claiming a vision had come to him in a dream. He tried to convince Pearl that she was the reason the house was suffering. That she needed to perform a ritual that he would guide her through."

Wei-wei's face heated. "I would have never thought…."

"Pearl wasn't fooled. She's dealt with all manner of sweet talkers, smooth talkers. But someone like Lady Bai, who is well-bred and sheltered—"

"I'm not so sheltered," Wei-wei insisted. Though perhaps she was. She would have never imagined such a scheme existed.

"After you realized the daoshi was a fraud, why didn't you take down the talisman?" Wei-wei continued.

"I wanted to," Song Yi confided. "But Mother is superstitious. She says the talisman might still have sorcery in it. Better not to tempt fate."

Wei-wei still had the daoshi's yellow paper as well. It was only a piece of paper, but why take chances? She'd burn it at the end of ghost month as a final send-off to the spirits.

"If you post that talisman, be careful," Song Yi warned. "It seems to serve as a sign to those imposters that someone trusting and vulnerable lives inside. You'll likely get a visit that same day with some outlandish story."

She didn't tell Song Yi there was no worry of any such visit. The daoshi was dead, but then Wei-wei remembered he had accomplices. Perhaps they were the ones who had plotted against him and caused his death.

Now that Wei-wei knew the nature of their swindle, preying on young women, she wanted to make sure they were caught and brought to justice. Well-bred and sheltered girls needed to protect one another any way they could.

Wei-wei hired a sedan to take her to the magistrate's yamen and raised her parasol above her to shield herself from the sun. They were in the heart of the summer season and the air was sweltering with heat. Maybe that was why wandering ghosts opted to travel during the seventh month, she reasoned. Ghosts were always cold.

They had reached the gates of the administrative building. Wei-wei paid the sedan runner before entering the courtyard.

A queue of petitioners filled the corridor that was situated between two rows of offices. From the rumble traveling through the crowd, Wei-wei surmised that there was a delay. The tribunal doors up front were closed which meant everyone was barred from appearing before the magistrate.

Wei-wei stood on her toes to see what was happening at the front of the line. There were angry voices and several of the clerks had come out to usher part of the crowd inside to file reports in the side offices.

Finally, the tribunal doors opened. Gao came striding out with a cadre of constables trailing after him. The look on his face was an outright scowl, which for Gao was unusual. She'd known his temper to be unfailingly steady, even in the worst of situations.

Gao saw her as he neared the gates and broke the formation to come over.

"Wei-wei," he began, lowering his voice. "The body. It's gone."

CHAPTER 7

"Are you certain he was dead?" Wei-wei asked, incredulous.

Gao ducked beneath her parasol, a comical sight considering how tall he was.

"Let's not start any rumors," he warned quietly.

"You said the constables thought he had moved."

Gao rolled his eyes. "I know dead, Wei-wei."

"They say that Daoist masters when they meditate can become so still that it's a state near death. Maybe that was what happened."

Gao directed her out through the gates and onto the street.

"He wasn't a Daoist master," Gao reminded her, speaking more freely now that they were outside the compound. "He was an imposter and a fraud."

Wei-wei took a deep breath and met Gao's eyes. "What exactly happened?"

She could see how the problem vexed him.

"The door of the coffin house was chained and locked last night," Gao reported. "This morning when the examiner came in, the body was gone. The chain was still on the door, nothing else had been disturbed."

A cold chill went down her spine. "Are there windows in the coffin house?"

Wei-wei wanted to believe there was a reasonable explanation. She had seen the trick knife and the fire powder, but there were things that happened during Daoshi Yu's presentation that she couldn't explain. The way his eyes had suddenly flashed red at her and the strange reflection of the daoshi she'd seen across the street.

"The windows are small and barred shut," Gao went on. "It's possible someone could have entered through one of them, but taking the body out would have been difficult. Why all the trouble?"

"It sounds like the stories of wutong," Wei-wei realized, heart pounding.

"Wutong?"

"Demons who prey on women."

She'd read about wutong in one of her collections of strange tales. The fantastic stories were written by scholars as a diversion and were popular among the literati. She told Gao what she'd learned at the House of Heavenly Peaches from Song Yi. How the daoshi had shown up there, trying to seduce one of the girls into some lascivious ritual. "Wutong are one-legged demons who ravish men's wives," she elaborated. "And the daoshi specifically targeted Yue-ying and me during the street performance."

Gao listened to the entire telling without comment. "That's not possible, Wei-wei," he replied finally and with extreme seriousness. "The daoshi had two legs."

He couldn't keep the corners of his mouth from twitching. Wei-wei narrowed her eyes sharply at him.

"I wasn't saying Daoshi Yu was an actual demon," she

countered. "He, and now someone else, appears to be perpetuating an illusion of dark magic."

"If a demon tried to harass my wife, I'd send him back to the eighteen hells two times," Gao vowed with a grin. "Thirty-six hells."

"You're the demon," she retorted grabbing hold of his chin which only caused his smile to widen.

Then he grew serious. "I do have work to do. Corpsestealing is an abomination and Magistrate Li wants this case resolved before a panic spreads through the city. Apparently, rumors of sorcery and soul-stealing can quickly escalate."

Wei-wei could see how that could happen. All of these mysterious occurrences had her grinding her teeth and looking around every corner. She was working hard to remain calm and rational.

"I don't want to return home," she protested when Gao suggested it. "I don't want to be alone."

"You know it's probably the sorcerer's accomplices who stole his body. Without the mysterious figure of Daoshi Yu, they have no fantastic lies to sell."

"A gang of corpse robbers roaming the city isn't comforting either."

She shifted to move her parasol to her other hand and Gao had to step back to avoid it swiping him across the face. Suddenly he grabbed hold of the edge of the parasol between his fingers.

"Wei-wei," he began, his eyes lighting.

"What is it?"

"A bamboo parasol. Painted yellow." His fingers played thoughtfully over the spines. "There was a woman outside of the inn where Daoshi Yu was found. I walked by her, but didn't think anything of it at the time. It was a seedy back alley. Why would a proper lady be there, with a parasol?"

"An accomplice?" she surmised.

Gao exhaled slowly. "Perhaps. I should go speak to the ladies of the Heavenly Peaches. They saw the sorcerer the night before his death."

"And I'll go to Mingyu's tea house," Wei-wei said.

She would at least have the company of Mingyu and Wu Kaifeng there. And the hot cup of tea she'd been denied at the Heavenly Peaches.

The plan took them both to different sections of the Pingkang ward. The smell of incense and burnt paper hovered in the air now and there were many offerings of food set out on the streets. Wei-wei carefully avoided the makeshift altars as she made her way to the Spring Blossom tea house. Even beggars would starve rather than touch food meant for the spirits.

The courtesans and entertainers of the pleasure quarter had come from all over the empire. Wandering ghosts would float rampant through an area where so many had been orphaned and displaced.

The sight of the yellow and red talisman above the tea house door made her skin crawl.

Inside, Mingyu was on her feet again and pouring tea. It was said that being with child made some women uncommonly beautiful. Wei-wei didn't know if that was true in Mingyu's case. She was already considered one of the most beautiful women in the city, but she seemed to have a sudden radiance about her. Mingyu's cool, ivory skin had taken on a warm, almost otherworldly appearance.

"You're feeling better," Wei-wei greeted.

Mingyu's smile alone explained why the tea house was always full. "Much better. The herbal medicines you and Yue-ying bought were very helpful."

The former courtesan invited Wei-wei to sit and brought her a cup of fragrant tea. She took a moment to breathe in the steam, but there was other business to attend to before relaxing.

"Is your husband about?"

"Kaifeng is in the kitchen. Do you need him for something?"

"I wanted to ask him to remove that talisman above your door. I've learned that it carries ill fortune with it."

Mingyu's pleasant expression suddenly darkened. "You couldn't be more correct. I'd forgotten it was even there. That cursed daoshi who gave Yue-ying the talisman came by this morning, trying to tell us that there were evil spirits in the tea house that needed to be exorcised."

The porcelain cup nearly slipped from Wei-wei's fingers. Hot tea splashed over her sleeve as she set down the cup with trembling fingers.

"That's not possible."

"I know. Unbelievable, isn't it? The gall of such interlopers."

"No, I mean it couldn't have been the same daoshi."

Mingyu frowned. "Dark beard. Strange eyes. Called himself Daoshi Yu. Yue-ying described him to me. She said he was rather overbearing to you."

"What do you mean by 'strange eyes'?"

Mingyu thought about the question. "I can't say for certain. I didn't spare him too much time before Wu Kaifeng chased him away, but there was something odd about his eyes."

Wei-wei sipped at her tea while Mingyu described the rest of the encounter. The daoshi had appeared early that morning, frightening the guests. He'd talked about Yue-ying and the red mark on her cheek to capture Mingyu's attention. Then he'd spun a wild tale of evil spirits surrounding the tea house and threatening everyone within.

"Including my unborn child," Mingyu said distastefully. "Kaifeng grabbed him and threw him out."

Wei-wei swallowed with difficulty, her mind racing. If Daoshi Yu had come here this morning, then who had Gao found dead at the inn?

She debated saying anything to Mingyu about the dead sorcerer and the missing body. Such a fright couldn't be good for her in her delicate condition.

"Are you alright?" she asked Mingyu. "It must have been awful, to be accosted like that."

"I've lived in Pingkang for most of my life," Mingyu said dismissively. "It's a place of strange happenings."

She poured herself a cup of tea and took a drink before continuing. "I will admit though, he did look frightening. His clothes were wrinkled and torn and there was something wrong with his leg. He was moving oddly. His face looked bruised, like it had been stricken. And the way he was asking for money for the exorcism."

Mingyu's eyebrows knitted thoughtfully.

"What is it?" Wei-wei asked.

"He sounded desperate. Like he truly was afraid of something—and it wasn't whatever ghosts he claimed were haunting my tea house. He was afraid of something very real."

WEI-WEI HURRIED through the lanes to the House of Heavenly Peaches, but Gao had already come and gone. From there, she ventured toward the center of the ward. The most illustrious courtesan houses like the Lotus Palace were located at the heart of the Pingkang li, surrounded by a bustling marketplace and local temples and shrines.

Mingyu's strange encounter with Daoshi Yu clung to her

like the dregs of a bad dream. It wasn't possible, yet it had happened. It had happened.

Wei-wei couldn't rid herself of the dawning horror that they were touching upon something dark and unknown. She had to find Gao and tell him.

But Pingkang was a large and crowded ward. Wei-wei stood on the main avenue staring as a river of people passed by on either side of her. She had no idea where to start looking.

On the side of the street, there was a raggedly looking street urchin selling bundles of joss paper. Wei-wei approached him slowly. She had seen Gao do something like this but didn't know how the method would work for her. The boy glanced up at her as she approached with eyes that took up most of his face.

"Boy," she said, holding out a copper coin. "Can you find Constable Gao for me?"

"There, Miss!" he replied, pointing over her shoulder.

She turned, half-expecting it to be a trick, but Gao was crossing the street toward her in long strides. Before she could turn back, the boy snatched the coin from her fingers and scampered off.

"Heaven and earth," Wei-wei murmured. If curses existed, then blessings must as well.

She ran the last steps toward him. "He has a double!"

"What is this?"

"During Daoshi Yu's performance, I saw a figure that looked like an exact image of the daoshi. At first, I thought it was a ghost or his spirit separated from his body."

Wei-wei knew it sounded like nonsense when she tried to explain it now, but she had been convinced at the time.

"It was just a man similar in height and build dressed in the same gray robes. The body you discovered wasn't Daoshi Yu, but his accomplice."

Gao paused, absorbing the information. "My clever wife," he murmured finally. "But why would Daoshi Yu steal the body rather than just disappear?"

"I don't know, but you can ask him when you catch him. He was at Mingyu's tea house just this morning."

Gao's eyes lit up. "How long ago?"

"Just several hours."

The imposter could still be in this very ward.

They returned to the tea house where Gao enlisted Wu's assistance and sent a messenger informing the magistrate.

"If the sorcerer is here and still breathing, we'll find him," he vowed.

Her husband knew these streets and these streets knew him. Wu Kaifeng had also patrolled the city when he was head constable. If the daoshi was hiding in Pingkang, the two of them would track him down.

While they waited for news of the manhunt, Wei-wei tried her hand at serving tea to give Mingyu some time to rest. It was harder than she thought. She scalded her hand once which was better than when she scalded a customer. Mingyu had to step in then and use her charm to smooth away the complaints.

Wei-wei wasn't used to running back and forth so much, but it did pass the time.

Several hours later, the same scrawny paper-seller who'd pointed Gao out to her poked his head into the tea house. "They found him!" he reported.

Wei-wei and Mingyu found Wu and Gao near the local shrine just as they were leading a man dressed in gray robes onto the constable's wagon. Daoshi Yu's hair had fallen free, giving him a wild, almost savage appearance.

"Is this the man you saw?" Gao asked her while the daoshi thrashed about in his grasp.

Wei-wei stood frozen in place. At that moment, the man

shook the hair from his face and she could see his eyes. Now that she knew to look, it was easy to see. The pupils were elongated, covering nearly the entire iris. They looked almost like the eyes of a cat.

Or the eyes of a snake.

CHAPTER 8

"*I'm a dead man. I'm already dead. If I don't leave, she'll kill me. I'm dead. I'm already dead....*"

Gao squeezed his eyes shut and laid his head back against the door to the holding cell. Despite the heavy barrier, he could still hear the sorcerer rambling from inside.

The rest of the staff in the magistrate's yamen had long retired for the day. The guards were stationed at their usual location at the entrance of the building, but Gao was not taking any chances. Not after a body had been stolen just the night before.

He'd put himself at the door to the imposter daoshi's holding cell and planned to make a stand there that would last the night. It wasn't very different from when Gao had been hired as an enforcer and lookout in front of the gambling dens in Pingkang. It had been a while since he'd needed to, but he was capable of remaining awake through the night when duty called for it.

"*I'm dead. If you don't let me go, I'm dead.*"

Just when he thought it was over.

It was a welcome sight when Wei-wei appeared holding a basket over one arm.

"Have you eaten?" she asked.

"Goddess," he replied.

She settled in beside him with her back also propped against the door. The basket held boiled sweet potatoes and sticky rice balls dotted with sesame. There was also a pot of tea which she poured for both of them.

"What did you find out?" she asked.

"The magistrate questioned him. I questioned him. This is all he keeps saying," Gao sighed.

"She'll kill me. I'm already dead...."

"Who is *she?*"

He sighed. "The nine-tailed fox."

"A fox spirit?" she asked incredulously.

"It's the only thing he said aside from this chant."

Wei-wei tilted her head to one side, listening. Daoshi Yu repeated his litany two more times before going quiet. It did almost sound like a ritualistic chant.

"Has he gone mad?" she wondered.

"He's not mad."

But Yu was afraid of something. When they'd found him, he appeared as if he'd taken a beating. His face was hidden behind purple bruises and he walked with a limp. Gao suspected his foot was broken.

It was the opposite of how Gao had found the double. The missing body didn't have a mark on it, yet was deceased. Daoshi Yu was alive, but had suffered a pummeling.

Magistrate Li had tried to ask the sorcerer about his accomplices, about his schemes, about his attempts to seduce women by drawing them into lurid rituals. None of it had yielded any answers.

"Li Chen will question him again in the morning," Gao

explained. "But he didn't react when he was asked about his dead counterpart or the missing body."

"This is all so strange," Wei-wei said with a shudder.

The night was warm, even out in the open air. Gao put his arm around her and she rested her head against the crook of his shoulder.

"You should go home," he urged after some time. "Get some rest."

"I want to stay."

Her mind was probably weaving a fantastic tale to explain everything that had happened. Wei-wei had an active imagination and a head full of stories that kept her up some nights even without ghosts and demons feeding on her fears.

For his part, he had to admit he didn't mind the company. Wei-wei burrowed against his side and the soft, warm scent of her skin surrounded him.

They had met at night. Their courtship, if he could call it that, had happened in the moonlight during Wei-wei's illicit excursions into the city in the evenings. There was something about being together like this, under such odd circumstances, that felt fitting.

"Isn't the nine-tailed fox a woman who takes the shape of a fox?" he asked.

"It's a celestial fox spirit that takes the shape of a woman," she corrected. "A nine-tailed fox is considered a good sign."

Again, no answers there. Only more questions. It seemed everyone was seeing spirits and demons lately.

"Maybe he's afraid of the nine-tailed fox because of all the women he's corrupted," Wei-wei suggested distastefully.

"There is nothing the magistrate can punish him for at the moment," Gao pointed out. "Li told me as much after interrogating him."

Daoshi Yu hadn't been accused of any theft. Other than a physical resemblance, nothing connected him to the dead body at the inn either. And even if the two were found to be accomplices, what wrong had been committed other than the false promise of sorcery?

He did have one lingering question that Wei-wei could answer. "Which one is the true Daoshi Yu?"

"Does it matter?" Wei-wei replied. "They both are part of the illusion."

"But which was the one you spoke to? The one who was found at the inn or the man who is inside this holding cell?"

She thought it over. "I don't know," she said, surprised at the realization.

The holding cell had been quiet for a long time now. Gao sat up straight, startling Wei-wei.

"What is it?" she asked sleepily. She had started dozing off in his arms.

"The sorcerer," he declared, alarmed. His gut instinct told him something had happened. Something *was* happening at that moment.

Gao shot to his feet and shoved the door to the holding cell open. It was empty.

There was a pit inside where prisoners were lowered before removing the ladder. Other than the door, the only opening to the cell was a small vent to let in air and light near the roof. He looked up to see a pale figure disappearing through it.

THERE WAS a fluttering sound overhead like the beat of birds' wings. That was the only sign Wei-wei could detect that someone had come and gone.

"Stay here," Gao told her as he ran from the building. She could hear him yelling instructions to the guards outside the entrance before they gave chase.

Wei-wei did as she was told. She stayed in the empty holding cell and inspected the pit below and the small opening above. The only way to escape would have been to fly.

A long time passed, at least it felt like forever, before she heard footsteps returning. When she went outside, however, all she saw were the two guards beneath the nearly full moon.

"Where's Constable Gao?" she asked them.

They looked questioningly at one another before returning their gaze to her. That look told her they had expected to find him here.

"Where did the constable go?" she demanded.

The guards tried to call her back and help her search all at once. The three of them had separated to search the streets surrounding the compound. Gao had gone down one lane. She hurried down that way now with the guards trailing after her.

"Did you see the prisoner? Did you see who took him?" she asked desperately.

"No, madame."

They had seen nothing. They might as well have been chasing a ghost.

"Gao!" she called out his name through the empty streets, her voice echoing off the stones. There was no reply.

Wei-wei slowed, trying to think while her heart pounded fearfully. Just a moment ago, she'd been in Gao's arms. Now the night had swallowed him up. He'd been consumed in the unfolding mystery.

After a while, the guards tried to call her back. Wei-wei was wandering now in circles, retracing her steps. A nightmare sense of time and place had taken over her. Where could Gao have gone? Where had Daoshi Yu gone?

There was a long, thin shape on the ground. Wei-wei bent

to retrieve it and discovered it was a length of silk, long enough to tie around her waist several times. Just ahead was a stone structure. She didn't know if she'd passed it before, but she went there now.

It was the large opening of a well, large enough for a man to fall into. The bottom of it disappeared completely into darkness.

"Gao, are you in there?" she shouted only to hear her own voice echoing hollowly back.

Gao was careful and quick on his feet. He knew these streets. He couldn't have fallen in there. He couldn't have.

She searched for a rock on the ground. Straightening, she dropped it into the well and listened for the sound of a splash below. There was nothing.

The guards had caught up to her and were warning her to be careful.

"Quiet!" she hushed, reaching down to search for a larger stone to try again.

This time her hands closed around something else. It was a wooden trinket with a loop of string attached. She ran her thumb over the carving and knew immediately what it was.

It was the amulet she'd given Gao. Zhong Kui, the slayer of ghosts.

CHAPTER 9

At some point, whoever or whatever had snatched the sorcerer from his prison had lost its hold on him. Gao found Daoshi Yu scrambling through the streets, dragging his injured foot behind him. He caught up to Yu as he was leaning over the stone lip of a well, as if catching his breath.

Gao had grabbed him and Yu had fought back, still protesting that *she* was going to kill him. Then suddenly the sorcerer was staring behind Gao, his eyes wild with fear.

Overhead, Gao could hear a fluttering sound, like a great kite in the wind. He started to turn when something solid collided against him, sending him tumbling into the well with Daoshi Yu. Gao was falling, grasping out for a hold when there was none.

Gao landed with a thud on the dry bottom, gasping for breath like a fish out of water. The impact had knocked the wind out of him.

In the darkness, he could hear Daoshi Yu fumbling to his feet and limping away.

Gao struggled to his feet, finally able to draw breath

again. He was in some kind of passageway. An irrigation tunnel, perhaps? The light of the moon above revealed the stone rim of the well above. Below there was nothing but darkness. The sorcerer's footsteps had faded away.

Let him run. There was nowhere for the sorcerer to go.

Gao directed his attention to figuring out how to get back up the well. The stone wall was smooth and impossible to grip. Calling out to the guards was no good. He'd have to wait until morning and hope for more foot traffic in the area.

That was when a scream pierced the air, echoing off the walls. It was the sorcerer and he was shouting at someone or something. The sound also told him the passageway was larger than he had thought. He took a few steps into the darkness and was surprised to see what looked like an orange glow in the distance.

It also would seem that he and Daoshi Yu were not alone.

He took his knife in hand and ventured toward the mysterious light.

Wei-wei woke up the next morning alone in an unfamiliar chamber. She had gone to Magistrate Li Chen in the middle of the night to tell him what had happened. He'd listened calmly even though she was barely coherent. Then he'd spoken to the guards who were equally confused by what had happened.

"We will send out a search party for the constable first thing in the morning," he promised her.

Li Chen then arranged for her to stay in the magistrate's residence. He lived there alone with a few attendants and there were empty chambers available for her to cry herself to sleep in.

Part of her had hoped to wake up with Gao beside her.

That happened occasionally in their home. Gao's duties would keep him out late and she would fall asleep worrying, but he was always there when she opened her eyes in the morning.

He wasn't there this morning and her heart sank even further.

The search party had already set out, but something told Wei-wei this problem wouldn't resolve itself so easily. There were peculiar forces at play here. She didn't know what they were, but she had to accept that they were extraordinary.

Wei-wei had gone to bed in her clothes and the pins in her hair had come loose in her sleep. She righted her appearance as best she could, smoothing out her robe and pinning her hair in a simple coil.

That was when she spied the long strip of silk she'd found the night before in the street. It was pale yellow, almost gold in appearance, and soft to the touch like flower petals. Finely woven silk like that was expensive. To find it discarded in the street was like finding that someone dropped a silver ingot and didn't care to go back to retrieve it.

Where had the silk come from? Had it been dropped last night?

She pondered the mystery of the silk sash the entire way home. The idea came to her as she stood before the door. Someone had been watching them in the holding cell. Were they watching still?

Wei-wei looped the silk around the lantern post in front of her house, hoping whoever had lost it would be looking for it. She was looking for them too.

When she went inside, the emptiness of the rooms overwhelmed her. Every corner of the house became a place where Gao wasn't.

One thing stood out, needling her like sand in her eye. The yellow talisman still lay on her writing desk. Wei-wei stoked a fire in the stove and shoved the talisman into it, watching the edges curl and blacken.

As soon as the paper became engulfed in flame, a knock came on the door. Out front stood a familiar sight—the little scraggly street urchin who had snatched her purse three days ago only to return it.

"Gao Taitai," he greeted. And then, "Please come with me."

WEI-WEI HAD ASSUMED INCORRECTLY that it was Gao's fearsome reputation that had protected her the morning of the ghost festival. As her scraggly guide took her through narrow alleyway after narrow alleyway, she came to realize that whatever had protected her was something else entirely.

The boy squeezed into a narrow gap between buildings. Wei-wei had to press herself to the wall to follow him and when she emerged, she saw a gateway to a courtyard residence. The entrance was wide enough for a carriage and the boy opened the gates to lead her inside. The courtyard garden was well-kept and there was a walkway leading to the main hall. Instead of entering, the boy stood to wait in the courtyard.

Wei-wei took her place beside him, staring at the open gate. "Do you know where my husband Gao is?"

"The one we are waiting for will be here soon," was all he would say.

As time wore on, the boy started to become more excited. He shifted his weight from one foot to the other and kept raising his head as he looked to the entrance. Finally, Wei-wei could hear the creak of wheels approaching.

An elegant carriage appeared, accompanied by several youths who looked to be thirteen or fourteen. Unlike the little street rat who had brought her there, the youths were dressed in clean, modest clothing.

The carriage pulled into the courtyard and came to a stop before them. One of the youths hurried to pull aside the curtain and a young woman dressed in flowing silks hopped from the carriage, and lifted a yellow parasol. Wei-wei was immediately stricken both by her beauty and the lithe way in which she moved. The youths who accompanied her fell into step behind her as she came forward.

The woman looked to be younger than Wei-wei, who was twenty-six years of age. Her hair was pinned with jewels and her dress was adorned with elaborate sashes and ribbons in the same pale gold as the length of silk Wei-wei had found. The tendrils of silk fanned out behind her, lifted by the breeze, as she walked.

The nine-tailed fox.

The boy who had been her guide bowed low as the woman approached, but it wasn't until Wei-wei bowed that she returned the courtesy.

"Lady Bai," she said, taking her arm as if they were long-time friends. "I have long wanted to make your acquaintance."

Wei-wei walked with her into the hall which had been arranged for a banquet. They sat side-by-side while the attendants poured wine and brought food.

"I have many questions," the woman said with a quirk of her lips. "How does a well-born lady come to be married to Gao the Knife?"

She had many questions? Wei-wei had a few of her own but she was still stunned by the sight of the mysterious woman and her small army of foundlings.

"I...I bribed the matchmaker," was all Wei-wei could think to say.

The woman's eyes sparkled slyly. "You are quite the scandal."

Wei-wei was convinced the woman was responsible for snatching the body from the coffin house as well as abducting Daoshi Yu from the holding cell.

"Are you doing all of this for vengeance? Has the daoshi wronged you?"

The woman's amused expression faded. Without the crafty smile, her face appeared older, more world-weary. Wei-wei wondered if she had been wrong about the woman's age after all.

"You are a lover of stories, Lady Bai. How do our stories typically end? A young girl in love, a young girl seduced, a young girl ruined. I was that young girl." Her eyes glittered like black jade. "As were you."

Wei-wei was taken aback. "But…I wasn't ruined."

Even as she said it, she realized many did believe she was ruined. She had turned down the prospect of marriage to Magistrate Li Chen, a more respectable prospect. She had married beneath her station. Her husband was a lowly constable and rumor had it that she only married him because she had been disgraced.

"Why are you not drowned at the bottom of some well, Lady Bai?" the woman in silk asked her seriously.

Wei-wei was still here because her family hadn't disowned her—though she had been certain at one point that they would. She was here because she had dared to want a life with Gao, who gave her a taste of not just love, but freedom.

"I've been very fortunate," was all Wei-wei was willing to admit to this strange girl.

"There are those who delight in pushing women onto their backs for their own pleasure. And then equally delight in pushing us into that well afterward. Who would miss such creatures?"

Her smile had returned, but this time it was carved from ice.

Wei-wei had no reason to be less afraid of the woman in the carriage than she'd been of the sinister Daoshi Yu and his accomplices.

"Gao, my husband, is not one of those men," Wei-wei said, forcing her voice to remain steady. "Do you know what has happened to him?"

The young woman drank her wine and plucked up a morsel from one of the plates to enjoy. Wei-wei clutched Gao's ghost-slayer amulet in her hand as she waited.

"Gao the Knife is also fortunate," the woman replied finally. "To have such a loyal wife."

A tiny flick of her fingers sent two of the youths running.

"Eat," the woman invited pleasantly. "Drink."

Wei-wei ate and drank out of politeness while her gaze continued to dart to the entrance.

"Did you know that Chang'an is a city built upon cities? Temples rest where palaces once stood. One could inhabit the same place where a princess, a villain, a wine merchant had once lived."

"Our family home was once the residence of a palace bureaucrat who was executed for treason," Wei-wei said.

She seemed to enjoy that bit of information. "In past dynasties, whenever an invading army marched on Chang'an, the Emperor would just abandon the city and declare another city the capital. Years would pass, regimes would fall, and a ruler would decide to make Chang'an the capital again."

"That is very interesting," Wei-wei replied dutifully. She glanced once more toward the entrance. There was no sign of the two youths who had left or of Gao.

"With the ancient imperial courts so intent on escape, imagine what sort of escape routes they might have built," the woman went on. "Where palaces once stood, one might find unknown passages—" She stopped herself and laughed. "Look at what you've done, Lady Bai. I feel so akin to you that I've said too much."

At that moment, there was a scraping sound in the corner of the room. The youths rose and hurried to the corner, lifting a trapdoor. To her surprise, Gao climbed up from the floor covered in dust.

Wei-wei broke decorum to run to him. "What happened? Are you hurt?" She reached for him, searching his face for answers.

Gao looked around, taking in the surroundings. "I was lost down below. Then someone lit a lantern which led me here. Are you safe?" he asked quietly, fixing his gaze on the young woman.

"Brother Gao. Lady Bai," she set down her wine cup and stood. "I have things to do, so I shall leave you now."

With that, she breezed past them and out of the main hall. Wei-wei hurried after her with Gao following closely behind.

"What about Daoshi Yu? Where is he?" Gao called after her. "And there's still the matter of a wrongful death."

The woman climbed nimbly onto the carriage. "What death? What body?"

She smiled coyly at them before letting the curtain fall.

Wei-wei and Gao watched as the carriage drove away. Then they returned to the banquet hall to also find it empty.

As the seventh month came to an end, Wei-wei set a basin of water out on their doorstep and gingerly floated the paper lotus lantern in it. Gao brought a taper to light the candle inside..

Throughout the neighborhood, up and down the lane, other households had done the same. The floating pink lanterns would burn into the night. Once they all went out, it was a sign the wandering ghosts had left them to peacefully return to the underworld.

As she took in the sight of the quiet lane dotted with lights, Gao rested his hand over the nape of her neck, his thumb circling slowly. The knots loosened beneath his touch and she took in a deep breath, deeper than she had allowed herself in a long time.

The wandering spirits would leave now. In a year, the same ghosts would return. Their paths were not meant to be resolved. If the Hungry Ghost Festival commemorated anything, it was that the lost deserved to be remembered.

Wei-wei closed the door and turned around to see Gao

had moved to her desk. He was reading the latest entry in her journal.

"*Chang'an was a city built upon cities. Temples rested where palaces once stood,*" he read aloud. "You're writing about what happened?"

"Only Mingyu and Yue-ying will read it. It's a perfectly strange tale. A riddle without an answer."

Gao had asked Magistrate Li to look into the courtyard and banquet hall where they had met the young woman and her army of foundlings. It belonged to an official in the Ministry of Rites who had been away from the city for the month.

There were no more signs of Daoshi Yu or his double, either. Due to the unusual chain of events, the magistrate's office had records of only one man. A dead man was identified as Daoshi Yu. Then, days later, a man was brought in alive. Also identified as Daoshi Yu.

And then Yu had been abducted from his holding cell that very night.

It was one of the magistrate office's rare failures. The case was left unresolved though she and Gao suspected the sorcerer would not be seen again.

"I suggested to Li Chen that he should devote his time to other cases," Gao confided to her.

She would have thought Gao would have wanted to seek out answers about the mysterious stranger who wielded some unknown influence over the streets he patrolled.

"So, everyone fears Gao, and Gao fears the woman in the carriage?" she asked.

"I just have the good sense to stay out of her way," he said, the corner of his mouth lifting.

Wei-wei smiled at her husband and closed her journal.

~

THE STORY CONTINUES in *Red Blossom in Snow,* Li Chen and Song Yi's story of forbidden love and tangled pasts. Read the excerpt included at the end of this book to start they journey through dark secrets and passionate yearning—in a world where the worst thing you can do is fall in love.

NEED MORE?

Wei-wei and Gao first meet in *The Liar's Dice* and their love story unfolds in *The Hidden Moon. Death of a Sorcerer* takes place in between *The Hidden Moon* and *Red Blossom in Snow.*

When I originally envisioned Wei-wei and Gao's story, I couldn't imagine them being able to find happily-ever-after in just one novel. Their pasts were so different. Gao had a dark past to come to terms with and Wei-wei, despite her rebelliousness, is a person who wants to do the right thing for those she loves.

At one point, I envisioned a secondary series of "Lady Bai Mysteries" that would also take place in the world of The Lotus Palace. Even though Wei-wei and Gao's central love story was explored in The Hidden Moon, there's still a lot more about their relationship that I was curious about, specifically what happens when an extremely wealthy and pampered princess actually sets up house with a rogueish, street hustler?

Death of a Sorcerer was a chance to tease some of that out in fun ways, one of those being that Wei-wei has only recently put her very educated mind to the task of cooking.

While part of the story is domestic, the other part, in contrast, is a fantastic tale in the tradition of the Tang Dynasty chuanqi. Wei-wei was inspired by these romantic and fantastic tales to disguise herself in her brother's clothing and venture out into the city in The Liar's Dice. Death of a Sorcerer continues this nod to chuanqi with references to the wutong demon and fox spirits. The capital city of Chang'an is featured in a few of these chuanqi. In these tales, the city becomes maze-like and mysterious, another character in and of itself.

As I was researching chuanqi, I discovered Yilin Wang's wonderful translation of "The Woman in the Carriage." This is a story I had seen referenced before, but never had read a full translation. The story was so delightful and I knew the mysterious woman in the carriage was exactly the sort of bold character that would inspire Wei-wei.

The story takes place in the Tang Dynasty and is attributed to author Huangfu (皇甫), which is a family name. Rather than have Wei-wei read this story, I decided to have her experience it.

To read the translation and more about Yilin Wang's work, you can visit her website at: http://yilinwang.com/the-woman-in-the-carriage.

EXCERPT FROM RED BLOSSOM
IN SNOW

Tang Dynasty China, 850 A.D.

Song Yi wasn't the most beautiful woman in the Pingkang li. She wasn't the most musically gifted, nor known for being the most captivating hostess. One didn't have to be famous to make a living in the pleasure quarter. In fact, being so well-known, so infamous could be a great disadvantage.

Such had happened to clever Li Jilan who composed poetry that received great praise until one set of lines was deemed subversive. She was sent to the executioner for treason. Captivating Mingyu had a circle of powerful admirers who ended up dragging her into their dangerous schemes.

To survive in Pingkang, one didn't have to be most or best. One simply had to have a compelling narrative. A story that was intriguing enough. Alluring enough. Provocative enough. And possess just enough ability to not slip into obscurity.

Song Yi had never wanted to attract a crowd of admirers. She had no need for dashing young men to fight over her, to die for her, to declare their never-ending love for her. She just needed a few steady and dependable patrons who liked her enough.

Steady and dependable was what they called Magistrate Li Chen. For a time, Song Yi had fancied that he liked her enough. But then he had disappeared, his favor collapsing like the waves, as they say.

She hadn't seen or heard from Li Chen for months until this very night at Director Guan's banquet, when she learned that an undemanding patron carried his own kind of curse.

The banquet was in its second hour and the half-moon had hidden behind a blanket of clouds. The only trace of it was a ghostly light behind the gray. With no moon visible to gaze upon, it should have been acceptable to close the doors so the three of them weren't freezing, but no one paid musicians so much thought. They were merely hired entertainers. Not bonded or enslaved, but not much higher in status.

Song Yi's fingers were stiff from the cold, but she plucked out a dancing melody on the strings of the guzheng nevertheless. Her courtesan-sister Pearl accompanied her with a softly penetrating counter-melody on the flute while Little Sparrow struggled to keep up on the erhu. Every time the girl tried to draw her bow smoothly over the strings, her shivering would interrupt the flow of the sound, creating a warble that Song Yi hoped the scholars in attendance would overlook.

The fashionable silk robes they wore to perform only made matters worse. The bureaucrats gathered warmly beside lit braziers and glowing lanterns within the banquet room while Song Yi felt the evening breeze through every thin layer of her robe.

Their three melodies wove around one another in a final circling dance before fading at the song's end. A voice cut into the silence. Their host, the illustrious Director Guan, was making a formal welcome and announcement.

"Oh good, poetry recitation," Pearl whispered with glee. "We can get a break."

Little Sparrow sprang to her feet. "I'm going to see if we can get tea!"

"Make it wine instead," Pearl suggested, grabbing the discarded erhu out of the way so Sparrow's robe wouldn't become entangled in it. The girl had already flitted off.

"Try not to make a face every time she plays a wrong note," Song Yi said gently. "Sparrow is trying to practice."

"Not nearly enough," Pearl said beneath her breath.

As the big sister of their courtesan house, it was Song Yi's responsibility to keep the peace as well as make sure Sparrow kept up with her training. Unfortunately the girl was easily distracted. She had pulled one of the director's retainers aside to speak to him with eyes wide and hands fluttering.

They were between the mid-autumn and winter festivals, but the cold weather seemed to be coming in early to Changan that year. Song Yi attempted to rub some feeling back into her hands. Warmed wine sounded wonderful.

"Oh look," Pearl whispered, excited. "It's your noble gentleman."

Song Yi's pulse skipped. Her heart pounded erratically, but she did not look. Instead, she fiddled with the wooden bridges that held the strings of her instrument. She knew exactly who the *noble gentleman* was.

She'd suspected Li Chen would be here tonight. Director Guan was well-known as the magistrate's benefactor.

"He's in uniform. So disciplined and *authoritative*," Pearl cooed.

Song Yi twisted at a tuning peg, which she really shouldn't do in the middle of a performance. So she twisted it back, tightening and untightening aimlessly. She was a fool for not preparing a better way to occupy herself.

The gathering wasn't large enough to hide. And why

should she hide? Li Chen was just someone she'd poured wine for over polite conversation. He wasn't even that highly ranked of an official. He hadn't so much as touched her hand.

Miraculously, she was no longer shivering. She was actually burning up. Or rather, her cheeks were burning. If she asked Pearl whether Li Chen was looking her way, Pearl would tease her mercilessly. Instead, Song Yi risked just a single glance, lifting her gaze then lowering it.

There was the dark-eyed and serious look she was so familiar with. Jaw squared, brow furrowed, shoulders straight. Li Chen's uniform, a forest green robe, draped over him in crisp, orderly lines. His hair was hidden beneath a black cap that tied beneath his chin.

He was not looking at her. Just as she was not looking at him. Their gazes slid just past one another.

Director Guan snatched Li Chen up and hovered over his protege with a protective air. As Guan made introductions, Chen nodded from one man to the next.

Li Chen wasn't unsmiling. He was merely focused. Song Yi had said as much to the others to defend him when they'd complained he was stiff.

She had seen what Li Chen looked like when that rigid expression softened and those eyes warmed. It had taken some time to get past his well-mannered reserve, but then he had stopped coming by. All of her efforts were wasted.

Song Yi returned her attention to her instrument, but not fast enough.

"Why so cold, Elder Sister?" Pearl asked.

Pearl only called Song Yi that when she wanted to taunt her.

"The magistrate will think you indifferent," her younger courtesan-sister went on.

"I *am* indifferent," Song Yi replied, running her fingertip lightly over a taut string. It hummed beneath her touch.

Pearl snorted.

"It looks like we'll have no tea or wine," Song Yi mused, looking to Sparrow who had become lost in a conversation with the young man. He was dressed in blue and gray scholar's robes. Sparrow was only sixteen and showed the boldness if not the refinement of a courtesan ten years her senior. Her quarry looked as if he were searching for a means of escape.

Song Yi used the excuse to spy on Li Chen again who was most certainly not acknowledging her. Furtive and meaningful glances were an entire language at gatherings like these. As were sweeping glances. Searching glances. Li Chen employed none of those. It was impossible not to look her way. The viewing portal which framed the uncooperative moon was right behind her.

So that was the way of it.

Some courtesans could play the abandoned lover to great effect, but Song Yi was never one for such scenes, and neither was Li Chen. They'd had only a short string of late-night conversations. He'd finally relaxed enough to recline on the seat in her parlor. They'd laughed together with heads bowed close, but never, ever touching.

She was pulling her strings too tight again. Pearl's all-knowing look faded.

"What a know-nothing bureaucrat," Pearl huffed with disdain as if that had been her intention all along.

"Maybe you should go rescue that poor scholar from Sparrow," Song Yi suggested.

Pearl immediately set her flute down to obey. Song Yi didn't have any sisters by blood, but she loved the two fate had given her.

After a few poems had been recited, they would be expected to play again. She stood as well to stretch out her legs and wander over to one of the braziers for warmth. Li

Chen wandered to the opposite side of the room. Could she get him to do that all evening? Swim about the chamber in circles like a carp to avoid her.

Such games were unbecoming of her. She was Song Yi of the House of Heavenly Peaches. Subtle, graceful, uncomplicated.

She had first met Li Chen at another banquet thrown by Director Guan He a year ago. Before that, she had only known the magistrate by reputation. He'd been appointed to the capital several years earlier. He was young for the post. Talented. Honest.

Song Yi had been playing another stringed instrument, the pipa, that night. It was simpler and required less focus than the guzheng. She had glanced up mid-song to find him watching, but not with the serious, penetrating gaze which he employed presently. His gaze had seemed far away, as if he were daydreaming. His eyes had widened with surprise when they met hers, and she'd smiled without meaning to.

She'd looked quickly away. The smile wasn't meant to be an invitation. It wasn't meant to be anything other than a smile, unrehearsed. Li Chen was supposed to be an exacting and relentless lawman, but in that moment, he had looked so...guileless. Like someone who hadn't seen enough of the world rather than too much of it.

He showed up at their doorstep two weeks later, asking about her. It turned out he was from Yu prefecture and had heard she was from there also. That first night they had spoken for hours until dawn. The sitting fees had cost him a month's wages. Even Mother had felt bad for him.

Old Auntie had cackled. "Radish boy! Probably thought he was going to get something if he just stayed longer."

Li Chen admitted later he hadn't meant to linger so long. He limited his next visits to exactly one hour. Pearl thought him uptight. Song Yi had thought Li Chen sweet. He was homesick.

Yet now he couldn't meet her eyes. Perhaps he was embarrassed by how much undue attention he'd paid her. He was the county magistrate with responsibilities and duties to attend to. Or he might have simply lost interest. Some scholars came to Pingkang to spend every last coin, while for others, the pleasures of the district were just a novelty that quickly faded.

Pearl returned to where they had left their instruments with a subdued Sparrow following behind her, eyes cast downward. Apparently, Pearl had scolded the younger Sparrow for something. Song Yi left the warmth of the inner chamber to go to them. It would be time to play again soon.

Li Chen was directly in her path now, deep in conversation with Director Guan. Song Yi didn't veer as far away as she could have. She passed by, close enough to detect the minute tightening of his jaw before she drew away.

His avoidance could also be fueled by shame, Song Yi realized with a pang in her chest. Visits to a courtesan house were a frivolous indulgence to someone like him. It didn't matter the reason, truly. She was experienced enough to know how to smooth over such cracks to allow him to save face. She didn't need for admirers to declare their undying love or to remember her in poems and laments.

If Song Yi had to describe her approach, she would say that it was practical. Her patrons served a purpose for the moment. Li Chen's evening visits, lovely as they were, had kept their house running and her sisters fed.

Song Yi had managed to hold a talented and honorable magistrate's interest for a brief period of time. It had to be enough.

It was probably better for Li Chen and for her that they didn't have to maintain the illusion for too long.

~

Fog settled thick over the streets of Changan. It wove through the falling darkness of the evening, transforming the lanes and alleyways of the capital city into a maze of spectral shapes. It hid Li Chen as he waited outside the courtesan house, gathering his courage.

The more he thought of it, the more he was convinced he had managed the banquet last night poorly. He knew how he was meant to conduct himself in the tribunal court and his administrative offices. He knew how he was supposed to conduct himself in courtesan houses like the House of Heavenly Peaches. Banquets where he was to mingle with bureaucrats and ranking officials on one side and interact with courtesans on the other created an undefined area of contention. Unfortunately, the code books didn't have any guidance on this.

He was saved from having to go up to the door when the person he'd come to meet appeared at the front of the house.

"Miss Song Yi."

She turned abruptly, searching through the fog.

"I didn't mean to startle you," he said, drawing closer.

"Magistrate Li," she greeted, letting out a breath.

They stood before one another, edges blurred by the surrounding mist. She wore a pale robe that made her seem to blend into the fog. Blue, he thought, or maybe gray.

Song Yi usually avoided the butterfly-bright colors favored by the other entertainers in Pingkang. The night before, she'd been clothed in the deepening blue of an evening sky, of twilight fading into dusk.

She had immediately drawn his attention. Song Yi didn't need flashy colors or flirtatious glances to do so. It was always her presence that pulled at him. She had a calming, soothing aura about her with darkly luminous eyes that were searching and thoughtful.

Chen's gaze strayed to the heavy cloak lined with fox fur about her shoulders. "You're going somewhere."

She pulled at the edges the garment. "I have an engagement tonight."

"Of course." He hadn't thought of that.

"It's good to see the magistrate…after so long."

Song Yi was looking up at him, her expression inquisitive. She was being kind. They'd spent several hours the night before in a banquet hall while he painfully tried to figure out the proper way to engage with her.

In many ways, the last months had been plagued by the same indecision.

They stared at one another, the silence stretching long between them.

Li Chen broke the silence first. "I could escort you. To wherever you're going."

She hesitated. "It's far away. Outside of Pingkang."

"I'll hail a carriage."

He turned to the street and raised his arm to wave down a passing transport, grateful to at least be of use. It wasn't long before a carriage came to a stop before them. Li Chen turned and offered his arm to help her up. She took hold of him only briefly as she stepped past him. The time apart had made them awkward around one another.

Song Yi turned once she was seated to look down at him. This wasn't going at all to plan—most likely because he hadn't made a plan.

"It was good to see you last night," he said, at last admitting it.

"Out of the corner of your eye?" she asked with a tilt of her head that wrecked him.

"Yes." The little laugh he gave was meant for himself.

"Even the most stuffy of bureaucrats could at least manage a sly glance," she chided.

He drew closer, his chest warming. "You looked well."

It wasn't what he'd meant to say. *Pretty* seemed too terse. *You looked like the only thing I ever wanted to see*, was inappropriate after their last parting had ended abruptly, without farewell.

"Where to?" the carriage driver asked impatiently.

"Chongren li," she replied.

"May I ride with you for a bit?" he asked in a rush.

The carriage had started forward before lurching to a halt.

Song Yi hesitated, her teeth worrying over her bottom lip, before she replied, "Of course, Magistrate."

She moved aside to allow him room on the seat. As the carriage started forward, they fell into silence once more. The fog hung all around them.

"I didn't forget you," he said, going immediately to the heart of the matter.

"Admirers come and go," she replied lightly.

"I know exactly how long it has been since we last spoke."

Her expression softened. When she looked at him like that, he couldn't remember why he'd ever tried to stay away.

He had been investigating the Incident at the Yanxi Gate, a high-profile assassination that led to threats to public officials and a series of murders in the city. Song Yi herself had received a warning that he was certain was meant for him. The danger was so imminent he'd used his authority as county magistrate to lock down the wards and put the city on curfew.

"I feared being seen with me would put you in danger," he explained.

But the danger was long settled by now. The Yanxi Gate conspiracy had been adjudicated months ago.

"I thought it was because you were about to be married," she replied.

Song Yi turned away to watch the buildings pass by. Lanterns formed dots of light that marked their path through the streets.

The carriage passed through the ward gates with nothing more than a few respectful nods from the city guards.

He had mentioned his potential betrothal to Song Yi, hadn't he?

"My family wishes for me to be married soon," he'd complained sullenly one night. It was late and he'd had more than a few cups of wine in Song Yi's sitting room.

The reveal had given her a moment's pause before she'd lifted the flask to pour him another cup. The movement caused her sleeve to pull back, exposing her bare and elegant wrist.

"It's a wonder you're not long married already, Magistrate," she'd said, in that soft silk voice that warmed his skin.

Marriage didn't necessarily prevent officials from visiting the courtesan houses, from courting song girls, from taking lovers, but Li Chen couldn't imagine dividing his intentions so. It would be courting disaster, not to mention disrespectful to his future wife. And to Song Yi.

But that business had also concluded long ago.

"The arrangement never came to be," he confessed.

"I know," Song Yi replied. "I heard."

When she looked back to him, the fading daylight cast her face in shadow. He could see the glint of lantern light in her eyes. Shapely, inviting, peach blossom eyes which were slender in shape, tapering toward the corners. Those lovely eyes watched for his reaction and he could see the questions gathered behind them. He hadn't known there was gossip about his failed betrothal. Then again, people tended to be careful what they said in passing around a magistrate.

"The heavy fog always reminds me of Yu prefecture," he said, looking into the swirl of gray around them. In terms of changing the conversation, it was an inelegant attempt. He was better at asking questions than answering them.

"The signal of the coming winter," Song Yi agreed. "When my family first arrived in Yuzhou, I thought we were at the edge of the world. The fog surrounded us, erasing the shoreline so there was no telling where heaven or earth began."

He loved listening to how she described the world.

"Like gray ghosts rising from the water," he remarked.

Song Yi fell silent. Why had he said that? Talk of his home sometimes made him melancholy, but he'd always been careful not to let their conversations drift that way.

"My mother sometimes said that," she revealed quietly. *"This is a place of ghosts."*

They had come from the same place. It was a part of their past they shared, and why he'd formed an immediate bond with her.

"I have a memory," he began. Song Yi leaned in to listen closely and he could smell her faint perfume. The creak of the wheels beneath them threatened to drown out his words. "A memory of a thick blanket of fog that covered everything one morning. Everything disappeared beneath it, the streets, the buildings, the people. I was studying in a library when I saw someone emerge from the mist. It was a girl."

"She was beautiful, of course," Song Yi teased, but only half-heartedly. He'd brought up bad memories with his talk of ghosts.

"She was," he paused, remembering. "She was searching for something. I've never forgotten the look on her face. Sometimes I wonder if the girl was real, or did I dream her?"

Song Yi shifted in the carriage seat. She'd probably heard many versions of this same story. *I saw you in a dream once. I dreamt of you before we ever met.*

Li Chen had thought of that strange memory the first time he'd seen Song Yi appear through a silk curtain, but he thought it best not to mention that now. He didn't want her to think of him as just another vapid admirer.

They had reached the gates of Chongren ward. Song Yi tensed beside him and he asked her if there was something wrong.

"Nothing's wrong," she said, followed by a deep breath. When she faced him again, she was smiling, but it was accompanied by a slight narrowing at the corners of her eyes.

"The Yanxi Gate assassination, it was brilliant how you solved that so quickly, Magistrate."

"It wasn't just me. In fact, it was hardly me at all."

"We all followed the stories in Pingkang, especially in the House of Heavenly Peaches."

Her smile had faded. The corners of her mouth tugged downward and her pretty eyes had become clouded, a dark sky in turmoil.

"Your constables arrested one of our patrons, General Lin Shidao's son. He was charged with treason."

"We were mistaken in that," he said quickly. "Lin Yijin was exonerated."

"Yes, of course. I wouldn't dare to criticize your office, Magistrate Li."

His heart pounded. "No, it's...I don't mind if you criticize me. I don't mind anything you say to me. I make mistakes all the time."

Song Yi appeared genuinely troubled. He asked her again if anything was wrong.

She bowed her head for a moment, then looked back at him. "I am really glad to speak to you again, Magistrate, but I really should have found a way to refuse when you asked to accompany me here."

Her smile this time was a mixture of joy and sadness. He realized she hadn't brought any instrument with her. She was dressed in a simple robe that, though pretty, wasn't meant to entertain.

She leaned forward to give instructions to the driver and they headed down a residential lane toward a gated house. The carriage slowed and it was obvious there were no banquet halls or drinking houses here.

The housekeeper came out to light the lanterns outside the gates. The posts were painted red as a sign of good fortune. The servant held the door open when he saw their approach.

"Lin Yijin was our best customer," Song Yi told him. "When he was charged with treason, no one wanted to come by anymore lest their own reputations be tainted. News of exoneration rarely spreads as quickly as news of scandal and ruin."

He started to tell her about all his office had done to make amends, but he held back. Nothing Song Yi said was untrue.

"Young Lord Lin has remained shut away since the ordeal and our house…hasn't seemed to recover either. We still are hired for engagements and our regular patrons still come by here and there and we have a few long-time friends—"

Chen nodded, hoping she would take that to mean she could stop explaining. He understood well enough now.

Soon the drums that signaled the closing of the ward gates would sound. As magistrate, he had authority to move freely through the city in the evenings, but Song Yi wouldn't be able to leave the ward to return to Pingkang until morning. Just after the sun came up.

It was that sort of engagement.

"This is the place," she said unnecessarily. The house inside the gate wasn't opulent, but it was a spacious residence with an inner courtyard encased in a surrounding wall. Not unlike the Li family manor in Yuzhou, but this was the capital. A house like this in the city either belonged to a family with a respected name or an official of modest rank.

"Thank you accompanying me, Magistrate Li," she said.

"It was—" He exhaled and met her eyes, unable to finish the sentiment.

Song Yi gave him a look that was not unkind.

If he hadn't stayed away for six months. If he had come to her immediately after his arranged marriage had fallen apart, would things be different?

They wouldn't have been. He knew that. He knew she had other patrons and admirers and that courtesan houses were expensive to run. The magistrate's office had access to every tax record, deed, and contract in the county.

Li Chen watched as Song Yi climbed down from the carriage to turn to the open gate.

"Will you be needing a carriage when you return?" he asked.

She shook her head, granting him one final, faint smile. He really should go now. Someone was waiting inside for her.

Li Chen directed the carriage driver to take him back to the administrative compound where he resided. Before they turned the corner, he glanced back to see Song Yi still at the gate, watching him as the carriage pulled away. Then she disappeared into the darkness of the evening, behind the clinging fog.

THE LOTUS PALACE MYSTERY SERIES

The Lotus Palace - Book 1

The Jade Temptress - Book 2

The Liar's Dice - novella - Book 3

The Hidden Moon - Book 4

Death of a Sorcerer - novella

Red Blossom in Snow - Book 5

THE GUNPOWDER CHRONICLES SERIES

Gunpowder Alchemy - Book 1

Clockwork Samurai - Book 2

Tales from the Gunpowder Chronicles - Book 3

The Rebellion Engines - Book 4

Steampunk short stories:

The Warlord and the Nightingale

Sign-up for Jeannie's mailing list (www.jeannielin.com) to receive updates on new releases, appearances, and special giveaways.